BETRAYERS

BETRAYERS

A Nameless Detective Novel

Bill Pronzini

A Tom Doherty Associates Book
New York

This is a work of fiction. All of the characters, organizations, and events portrayed in this novel are either products of the author's imagination or are used fictitiously.

BETRAYERS: A NAMELESS DETECTIVE NOVEL

Copyright © 2010 by the Pronzini-Muller Family Trust

A Forge Book
Published by Tom Doherty Associates, LLC
175 Fifth Avenue
New York, NY 10010

www.tor-forge.com

Forge® is a registered trademark of Tom Doherty Associates, LLC.

ISBN 978-0-7653-1820-6

First Edition: July 2010

Printed in the United States of America

0 9 8 7 6 5 4 3 2 1

For Elisa and Michael Seidman

BETRAYERS

1

TAMARA

The tests came back negative.

He hadn't given her AIDS or any other STD.

Her first reaction was relief, naturally, big relief. The way Vonda and Ben had talked about Lucas Zeller, Tamara had started picturing him as a walking germ factory capable of infecting the whole damn city. Scared, all right. More scared than she'd ever been in her life during that endless two-week wait for the test results.

When the relief wore off, she got mad all over again. At herself to begin with, for having unprotected sex with a virtual stranger. Only once out of the six times they'd got it on, but once was one too many. Stupid. As stupid as you could get in a city like San Francisco, where STDs were rampant, where thousands had suffered and died in the AIDS scourge.

No mystery about why she'd rolled over so quick and easy for somebody she hardly knew. Almost a year since Horace had deserted her, almost a year since she'd last gotten laid, and Lucas had seemed all right, intelligent, cool, nice quiet eyes, gentle way about him, and he hadn't come on strong when they met at Vonda and Ben's wedding reception or when he called her up the next week. *She* was the one who practically dragged him into her bed that first night. Lord, she'd been horny . . . but that was no excuse. She should've known better. She did know better. Fool!

Then she started thinking about the phone conversation she'd had with him, the day after Vonda told her he was part of one of those secret little fraternities of black men, most of them married, who got together now and then to drink, maybe smoke some weed, and have casual sex with one another. Closet bisexuals who refused to admit they had a gay side. If the AIDS scare hadn't been enough to bust up her brief relationship with Lucas, him being on the down low would've done it. That and the phone conversation. Thinking about it made her even madder. At him again, this time.

The only phone number she had for him belonged to his creepy mother, Alisha . . . if she was his mother. And he hadn't given it to her; she'd gotten it from the redial on her home phone, after he used it to check in with Mama the second night she slept with him. So she'd called up, mad and scared, and he'd been there, and she'd slammed into him, hard. Didn't faze him a bit. He came back at her all cool and offhand and slick as grease.

"You shouldn't jump to conclusions, Tamara. None of it's true."

"Oh, so you're not on the down low."

"Of course not. Even if I was, don't you think I'd be very careful, take precautions?"

"I don't know. I don't know you, man."

"Rest easy. I had myself tested not long ago, but not for that reason. I'm sexually active and mistakes happen. You ought to know that. You're the one who was ready and eager to do it that once without a condom."

"You wanted it as bad as I did."

"Come on, now. Lighten up, quit worrying. Everything's cool."

"Yeah, sure. James swears you tried to get him into a switch-hitters' club."

"Wrong. A sports fan club, that's all."

"He says different. He says you came on to him."

"He's either mistaken or lying."

"Why would he lie?"

"I don't know. Grudge thing, maybe. He didn't like it that I went to his sister's wedding reception. Claimed he didn't invite me, but that's a lie, too."

Vonda's ex-gangbanger brother James was a lot of things, including a racist, but he wasn't a liar. And the only grudges he'd ever held were against other gangbangers and white folks.

"I don't believe you, Lucas," Tamara said.

"That's too bad."

"Yeah, too bad for both of us if my test comes back positive."

"It won't."

"It better not. Or I'll damn quick report you to the Department of Health."

"So I guess this means you don't want to see me anymore." Real casual, as if he'd said it through a yawn.

"You better believe it. Sex was all we had, and no way I let you dip your dumbstick in me again."

His creepy mother was listening. Tamara heard Mama say something in her deep, scratchy old voice but couldn't make out the words.

"Oh, hell," he said, "I know it. You were right as usual."

Talking to Mama. Then, to Tamara, "How'd you get this number?"

"What? What do you care how I got it? I run a detective agency, remember?"

"Oh, I remember. My bad. I shouldn't have taken the chance with you."

"What the hell does that mean?"

"Good-bye, Tamara," he said. And he banged the receiver in her ear before she could do the same to him.

Made her skin burn hot, remembering.

When she told Vonda about the test results, she got the advice she expected: let it end right there. Good advice, too—for most women. You dodge a bullet, the smart thing is to chalk it up to experience and get on with your life. Only she wasn't made that way. He'd used her, scared her, made her feel bad about herself just when she'd been starting to get her stuff together again; she was entitled to one last shot at him.

She called Mama's number again, and this time it was no longer in service. That didn't stop her. She knew where Lucas worked and she had his home address, or thought she did, because back when they first hooked up she'd run a superficial background check on him, out of curiosity and because he'd said some things that made her wonder if maybe it wasn't his mother he lived with but a wife. Tamara probably wouldn't have done it if their relationship had been the kind that might turn serious, the kind built on caring and trust, but they'd both made it plain from the get-go that their only interest in each other was what went on between the sheets.

The b.g. check had reassured her . . . then. Lucas Zeller had a clean record. Squeaky clean, in fact. Thirty-four, unmarried, worked as a salesman for an electronics company in the East Bay, lived here in the city, had never been arrested or in trouble of any kind. The only mark against him, or so she'd thought then, was that he was a mama's boy.

So if she couldn't get him on the phone, then she'd confront him in person. Company he worked for was Dale Electronics in El Cerrito. He'd told her he spent a lot of his time on the road, but he happened to be in his office the day she went over there. She expected to have some trouble getting in to see him, but that didn't happen. She just walked right in.

Yeah. Like walking into a wall.

She'd never seen the man at the desk before.

Different guy. The *real* Lucas Zeller.

Superficial resemblance, nothing more. Dark skinned, where her man had been light skinned and claimed to have white blood—a fudge swirl. Round head instead of blocky, straight nose instead of hooked, all his hair instead of a receding hairline, and a smaller, neater mustache.

He looked at her business card, looked at her, flashed a thin, hopeful smile, and said, "Are you here about the theft?"

"Theft?"

"My wallet and briefcase. A month ago."

That put an end to her surprise. Tight-mouthed, she asked him where the theft had happened.

"Bertolini's, in the city. That's not why you're here?"

"Not exactly."

"Damn. I keep hoping at least the briefcase will turn up. I had some important papers in there."

"You see who took it?"

"No. I was there for drinks after work with some business associates . . . they didn't see anything, either. Must have happened while I was in the bathroom. I didn't even miss it until we were ready to leave." Heavy sigh. "I should've watched it more carefully. My wallet was in there, too." He added ruefully, "I thought it'd be safer than in my coat pocket."

"Lose much money?"

"There wasn't much in the wallet. But the thief made two ATM withdrawals from my checking account before I could close it. Six hundred dollars." He sighed again. "I had my PIN number in the wallet, too, because I keep forgetting it."

"Credit card charges?"

"No, thank God. I got them all canceled in time."

Tamara gave him a detailed description of the phony Lucas. "You know that man, Mr. Zeller?"

"No."

"See anybody looks like him the night your briefcase was stolen?"

"No, I'm sure I didn't. You think he's the thief?"

"Probably. He's the man I'm looking for, not you."

"I don't understand. . . ."

"He's been posing as you, using your name."

"What? Why would he do that?"

"Keep his own identity secret. Some other reason, too, maybe."

"Such as what?"

"I don't know yet."

"A scam? Oh, Christ, my job, my reputation . . ."

"You report the theft to the police?"

"Yes. Of course."

"Then you don't need to worry. He'd expect you to, and he knows you closed your bank account and canceled your credit cards. All he's doing is using is your name, and maybe your driver's license if he needs to show ID. He looks enough like you to pass."

"Should I report this to the police, too?"

"You can, but there's nothing they can do until he's ID'd."

"Then you don't have any idea who he is?"

"No, but I'll find out. You can count on that, Mr. Zeller."

Now she was *really* pissed. The phony Lucas was a property and identity thief in addition to being a slick, lying, manipulative switch-hitter. And what else? Scam artist, using the real Lucas Zeller's name to run a con of some sort? Wouldn't surprise her. Small-time grifter in any case, the kind that was always on the hustle, always looking for a quick and easy score. Big-time scammers wouldn't risk swiping a briefcase and six hundred bucks from ATM machines.

I shouldn't have taken the chance with you. Now she understood what he'd meant by that. She'd as much as said it herself, when he asked her how she'd gotten Mama's phone number. *I run a detective agency, remember?* All just a spicy game for him, laying a woman who worked on the right side of the law. In a way, that was more galling to her than any of the rest. She hadn't even been human to him; all she'd been was a sex object, no more real to him than a piece of meat.

And what about Alisha? Really his mother? Girlfriend, wife? Whoever she was, she couldn't be ignorant of any of the games he played. Grifter herself, likely. They might even be a team, working separately or together.

Tamara thought about fessing up the whole ugly business to Bill, bringing him and Jake Runyon into the hunt. Even considered going to Pop because of his connections at the Redwood City PD. But she ended up not telling any of them. Bill would be sympathetic, nonjudgmental, but she was too embarrassed to face him with her stupidity unless absolutely necessary. Pop would go ballistic; she'd never have a minute's peace. Besides, it was personal. And she knew almost as much as they did about how to find somebody who didn't want to be found, didn't she? More, when it came to using the Net.

Sure, fine. Except that she couldn't get a line on the man.

She tried everything she could think of, but the available data was just too sketchy. Trying to trace the phone number she had for Mama was a dead end: no record of the number, so no user's address. One of those GoPhones that had a built-in number and limited amount of call minutes and that didn't have to be registered. James had told Vonda he didn't know how the man could be reached except by phone. And even if she had that number, there'd be no point checking it; it'd just turn out to be another GoPhone and probably out of service by now, too.

She knew what kind of car he drove, had ridden in it on their first date—a five-year-old light brown Buick LeSabre. It had a scrape and dent on the right front fender, the result of a minor accident, he'd told her; she'd noticed that, but she hadn't paid any attention to the license plate. No reason she should have. You go out on a date, you're interested in the man, focused on him, not details about his ride.

Was he still in the city, the Bay Area, California? No way of knowing. Her phone call, Mama reminding him of the mistake he'd made messing with a detective, could've been enough to send both of them packing. Chances were he was a floater anyway, moving to fresh territory every few weeks to stay one jump ahead of the law. For all Tamara knew he was in L.A. or Miami or New York by now.

On the other hand, he could be the reckless type, overconfident enough to hang on in the city or the Bay Area. Say he was working a con and had a sucker on the hook—that might keep him here until he made his score. In that case, would he keep on using Lucas Zeller's ID? She hoped so. If he was using a different name now, he'd be even harder to track down.

She got in touch with Felice, her contact in the SFPD's computer department, and talked her into checking local, state, and federal files for known African American thieves and grifters who answered his description and operated with an older woman who might or might not be his mother. Two possibles came out of that, but neither turned out to be the phony Lucas. Evidently he'd been lucky and hadn't had been busted . . . yet.

Tamara talked to several of the sixty or so people who'd been at Ben and Vonda's wedding reception—trying to get a handle on why he'd gone there. Not to see James, who'd been pissed when he showed up uninvited. To meet somebody else? Cruising for victims or a male or female bed partner? Nobody had any answers or leads to his whereabouts. Most didn't remember him, and the ones who did hadn't seen or talked to him since and couldn't tell her anything about him she didn't already know.

That left her with one other option: a face-to-face with James, a prospect that didn't appeal to her any more than it would to him. Hostile witness. Man hadn't wanted anything to do with her since he'd tried to hit on her back in his gangsta days and she'd blown him off and wounded his pride. Liked her even less, he'd told Vonda, after she'd gone to work for a white detective. It wouldn't be easy dealing with James, if she could get him to talk to her at all. They were like a couple of pieces of flint whenever their paths crossed: friction and sparks.

And if she couldn't get anything useful out of James? Well, she'd figure something out. No way that slippery bastard Lucas would get away with walking into her life, turning it upside down again, and then walking out free and clear to mess up somebody else's. Somehow she'd find him, find out his real name. No matter where he was. No matter how long it took.

And then she'd be there, front and center, when a cell door slapped his sorry black ass on the way inside.

2

There's a short story by John D. MacDonald called "I Always Get the Cuties," about a cop named Keegan whose specialty is solving cases in which amateurs devise elaborate plans to commit the perfect crime. He calls them his "favorite meat." They're a lot easier to work on, he says, than cases involving professional criminals.

Seems like I always get the cuties in my profession, too. Different kinds than Keegan's, but cuties nonetheless. Only they're not my favorite meat by any stretch. Give me a simple skip-trace, insurance claim investigation, employee background check, or any of the other routine jobs that make up the bulk of the agency's caseload. But for some reason, we seem to draw more than our fair share of the cuties, and even though I'm semiretired now, they usually fall into my lap. Screwball stuff. Like the one where a successful and seemingly rational businessman suddenly began attending the funerals of strangers for no apparent reason. Or the one I'd had recently that started off with the allegedly impossible theft of some rare and valuable mystery novels and ended up with cold-blooded murder in a locked room. Keegan would have loved that.

Or the one that had walked into the agency offices this morning.

A new cutie with seriocomic overtones, no less. A little of this and a little of that all mixed together into what was bound to be a not very appetizing stew. City bureaucracy, real estate squabbles, nocturnal prowlings, petty vandalism, threatening phone calls, poisoned cats, and, ah yes, one more ingredient that had been left out of the recitation of the original recipe . . .

Young man," Mrs. Abbott said to me, "do you believe in ghosts?"

The "young man" surprised me almost as much as the question. But then, when you're eighty-five, a man in his early sixties can seem relatively young.

I said politely, "Ghosts?"

"Poltergeists, malevolent spirits?"

"Well, let's say I'm skeptical."

"Loved ones from the Other Side?"

"Likewise."

"I've always been skeptical myself. But I can't help wondering if it might be a ghost who is responsible for all that has happened."

Beside me on the sofa, my client, Helen Alvarez, age seventy and likewise a widow, sighed and rolled her eyes in my direction. She hadn't mentioned ghosts in my office; this was the ingredient that made the cutie even cuter.

She smiled tolerantly across at Mrs. Abbott in her Boston rocker. "Nonsense. When did that notion come into your head?"

"Last night. I've been reading a book."

"A book? What book?"

"About spirit manifestations and the like. It's quite a fascinating concept."

"It's a load of crap," Mrs. Alvarez said.

"I can't imagine why a poltergeist would suddenly invade my home. Carl, on the other hand . . . well, that does seem possible."

I said, "Carl?"

"My late husband. His shade, you see."

Mrs. Alvarez emitted an unladylike snorting sound.

"Don't you think it's possible, Helen?"

"No, I certainly don't. Carl has been gone ten years, for heaven's sake. Why would his spirit come back *now*?"

"It could be he's been angry with me since he passed over."

"Why would he be angry with you?"

"I'm not sure I did all I could for him when he was ill. He may blame me for his death—he had a nasty temper, you know, and a tendency to hold a grudge. And surely the dead know when the living's time is near. Suppose he has crossed over to give me a sample of what our reunion on the Other Side will be like?"

There was a small silence.

Mrs. Alvarez, who was Margaret Abbott's neighbor, friend, watchdog, and benefactor, shifted her long, lean body and said patiently, "Margaret, ghosts can't ring the telephone in the middle of the night. Or break windows. Or dig up rosebushes."

"How do we know what spirits can or can't do? Perhaps if they're motivated enough . . ."

"Not under any circumstances. They can't put poison in cat food, either. Now you *know* they can't do that."

"Poor Spike," Mrs. Abbott said. "Carl wasn't fond of cats. He used to throw rocks at them."

"It wasn't Carl or his spirit or anybody else's spirit. Living people are behind this deviltry and you and I both know who they are."

"We do?"

"Of course we do. The Pattersons."

"Who, dear?"

"The Pattersons. Those real estate people."

"Oh, I don't think so. Why would they poison Spike?"

"Because they're vermin. They're greedy swine."

"Helen, dear, don't be silly. People can't be vermin or swine."

"Can't they?" Mrs. Alvarez said. "Can't they just?"

I put my cup and saucer down on the coffee table, just hard enough to rattle one against the other, and cleared my throat. The three of us had been sitting here for about ten minutes, in the pleasantly old-fashioned living room of Margaret Abbott's Parkside home, drinking coffee and dancing round the issue that had brought us together. All the dancing was making me uncomfortable; it was time for me to take a firm grip on the proceedings.

"Ladies," I said, "suppose we concern ourselves with the facts. That'll make my job a whole lot easier."

"I already told you the facts," Mrs. Alvarez said.

"I'd like to hear them from Mrs. Abbott as well. I want to make sure I have everything clear."

"Yes, all right."

I asked Mrs. Abbott, "This late-night harassment started two weeks ago, is that right? On a Saturday night?"

"Saturday morning, actually," she said. "It was just three a.m. when the phone rang. I know because I looked at my bedside clock." She was tiny and frail and she couldn't get around very well without a walker, and Mrs. Alvarez had warned me that

Mrs. Abbott was inclined to confusion, forgetfulness, and occasional flights of fancy. At least there didn't seem to be anything wrong with her memory today. "I thought someone must have died. That is usually why the telephone rings at such an hour."

"But no one was on the line."

"Well, someone was breathing."

"Whoever it was didn't say anything."

"No. I said hello several times and he hung up."

"The other three calls came at the same hour?"

"More or less, yes. Four mornings in a row."

"And he didn't say a word until the last one."

"Two words. I heard them clearly."

" 'Drop dead,' " Mrs. Alvarez said.

"Yes. It sounds silly, but it wasn't. It was very disturbing."

"Can you remember anything distinctive about the voice?" I asked.

"Well, it was a man's voice. I'm certain of that."

"But you didn't recognize it."

"No. It was as if it were coming from . . . well, the Other Side."

Helen Alvarez started to say something, but I got words out first. "A long way off, you mean? Indistinct?"

"Yes, that's right."

Muffled. Disguised. "Then the calls stopped and two days later somebody broke the back porch window. Late at night again."

"With a rock," Mrs. Abbott said, nodding. "Charley came and fixed it."

"Charley?"

"My nephew. Charley Doyle. Fixing windows is his business, you see. He's a glazier."

"And after that, someone spray-painted the back and side walls of your house."

"Filthy words, dozens of them. It was a terrible mess. Helen and Leonard cleaned it up."

"Leonard is my brother," Mrs. Alvarez said, purse-lipped. "It took us an entire day."

"Then my rosebushes . . . oh, I cried when I saw what had been done to them. I loved my roses. Pink floribundas and dark red and orange tears." Mrs. Abbott wagged her white head sadly. "He didn't like roses any more than he did cats."

"Who didn't?" I asked.

"Carl. My late husband. And he sometimes had a foul mouth. He knew all those words that were painted on the house."

"It wasn't Carl," Helen Alvarez said firmly. "There are no such things as ghosts; there simply *aren't*."

"Well, all right. But I do wonder, dear. I really do."

"About the poison incident," I said. "That was the most recent happening, two nights ago?"

"Poor Spike almost died," Mrs. Abbott said. "If Helen and Leonard hadn't rushed him to the vet, he would have."

"Arsenic," Helen Alvarez said. "That's what the vet said it was. Arsenic in Spike's food bowl."

"Which is kept inside or outside the house?"

"Oh, inside," Mrs. Abbott said. "On the back porch. Spike isn't allowed outside. Not the way people drive their cars nowadays."

"So whoever put the poison in the cat's bowl had to get inside the house to do it."

"Breaking and entering," Mrs. Alvarez said. "That's a felony, not a misdemeanor. I looked it up."

"Yes, it is."

"Not to mention the final straw. That's when I decided it was time to hire an investigator. The police weren't doing a thing, not a thing."

She'd told me all that before. I nodded patiently and asked, "Were there any signs of forced entry?"

"Not that Leonard and I could find."

Mrs. Abbott said abruptly, "Oh, there he is now. He must have heard us talking about him. He's very sensitive that way."

I looked where she was looking, off to one side and behind where I was sitting. There was nobody there. I almost said, *You don't mean your dead husband's ghost,* but changed it at the last second to, "Who?"

"Spike," she said. "Spike, dear, come and meet the nice man Helen brought to help us."

The cat that came sauntering around the sofa was a rotund and middle-aged orange tabby, with wicked amber eyes and a great swaying underbelly that brushed the carpet as he moved. He plunked himself down five feet from where I was sitting, paying no attention to any of us, and began to lick his shoulder. For a cat that had been sick as a dog two days ago, he looked pretty fit.

"Mrs. Abbott," I said, "who has a key to this house?"

She blinked at me behind her granny glasses. "Key?"

"Besides you and Mrs. Alvarez, I mean."

"Why, Charley has one, of course."

"Any other member of your family?"

"Charley is my only living relative."

"Is there anyone else who—*uff!*"

An orange blur had come flying through the air and a pair of meaty forepaws nearly destroyed what was left of my manly pride. The pain made me writhe a little, but the movement didn't dislodge Spike; he had all four claws anchored to various portions of my lap. I thought an evil thought involving retribution, but it died when he commenced a noisy purring. Like a fool I put forth a tentative hand and petted him. He tolerated that for all of five seconds. Then he bit me on the soft webbing between my thumb and forefinger, jumped down, and streaked wildly out of the room.

"He likes you," Mrs. Abbott said, smiling.

I looked at her.

"Oh, he does," she said. "It's just his way with strangers. When Spike nips you, it's a sign of affection."

I looked down at my hand.

The sign of affection was bleeding.

One of those cases, all right. A bigger cutie, in fact, than I'd anticipated after Helen Alvarez started laying it out for me in my office. I'd tried to avoid taking it on, but Jake Runyon and Alex Chavez had been out on other business and Tamara was sympathetic to Mrs. Alvarez, so I had no backup. No backbone, either, when it comes to this kind of case. How do you turn down a determined seventy-year-old widow with a problem neither the police nor most other private agencies will touch?

Mrs. Alvarez was not someone who listened to "no" when she wanted to hear "yes." She pleaded; she cajoled; she gave me the kind of sad, anxious, worried, reproving looks elderly women cultivate to an art form—the kind calculated to make you feel heartless and ashamed of yourself and to melt your resistance faster than fire melts wax.

I hung in there for a while, waffling, but Tamara put an end to my resistance. She'd established, with my blessings, an agency policy of taking on pro bono cases for individuals and small businesses who couldn't afford our fees—a worthwhile public service designed mainly for the benefit of ethnic minorities. Helen Alvarez was not really a minority, being an Angla married to a deceased Latino, and not exactly indigent, but that didn't make any difference to Tamara. She said we'd take the case, in a no-nonsense voice, and that took care of that. She'd been in a grumpy, distant mood for the past couple of weeks, snapping and growling when something went wrong or she didn't get her way, and arguing with her when she was like that was useless. The Good Tamara was on vacation. The Bad Tamara who sometimes replaced her was a pain in the ass.

So I'd listened to Helen Alvarez's tale and written down all the salient facts and agreed to interview Margaret Abbott. Mrs. Abbott's woes had begun three months ago, when Allan and Doris Patterson and the City of San Francisco had contrived to steal her house and property. The word "steal" was Mrs. Alvarez's, not mine.

It seemed the Pattersons, who owned a real estate firm in the Outer Richmond, had bought the Abbott property at a city-held auction where it was being sold for nonpayment of property taxes dating back to the death of Mrs. Abbott's husband in 2000. She refused to vacate the premises, so they'd sought to have her legally evicted. Sheriff's deputies declined to carry out the eviction notice, however, after a Sheriff's Department administrator went out to talk to her and concluded that she was the innocent victim of circumstances and cold-hearted bureaucracy.

Margaret Abbott's husband had always handled the couple's finances; she was an old-fashioned sheltered housewife who knew nothing at all about such matters as property taxes. She hadn't heeded notices of delinquency mailed to her by the city tax collector because she didn't understand what they were and hadn't sought to find out from her nephew or Mrs. Alvarez or anyone else. When the tax collector received no response from Mrs. Abbott, he ordered her property put up for auction without first making an effort to contact her personally. House and property were subsequently sold to the Pattersons for $286,000, about a third of what they were worth on the current real estate market. Mrs. Abbott hadn't even been told that an auction was being held.

Armed with this information, the Sheriff's Department administrator went to the mayor and to the local newspapers on her behalf. The mayor got the Board of Supervisors to approve city funds to reimburse the Pattersons, so as to allow Mrs. Abbott to keep her home. But the Pattersons refused to accept the reimbursement; they wanted the property and the fat killing they'd make when they sold it.

They hired an attorney, which prompted Helen Alvarez to step in and enlist the help of lawyers from Legal Aid for the Elderly. A stay of the eviction order was obtained and the matter was put before a superior court judge, who ruled in favor of Margaret Abbott. She was entitled not only to her property, he decided, but also to a tax waiver from the city because she lived on a fixed income. The Pattersons might have tried to take the case to a higher court, except for the fact that negative media attention was harming their business. So, Mrs. Alvarez said, they "crawled back into the woodwork. But if you ask me, they've come crawling right back out again."

It was her contention that the Pattersons were responsible for the nocturnal "reign of terror" against Mrs. Abbott out of "just plain vindictive meanness. And maybe because they think that if they drive Margaret out of her mind or straight into her grave, they can get their greedy claws on her property after all." How could they hope to do that? I'd asked. Mrs. Alvarez didn't know, but if there was a way, "those two slimeballs have figured it out."

That explanation didn't make much sense to me. But based on what I'd been told so far, I couldn't think of a better one. Margaret Abbott lived on a quiet street in a quiet residential neighborhood; she seldom left the house anymore, got on well with her neighbors and her nephew, hadn't an enemy in the world or any money or valuables other than her house and property that anybody could be after. If not the Pattersons, then who would want to bedevil a harmless old woman? And why?

Well, I could probably rule out Spike the psychotic cat and the malevolent spirit of Mrs. Abbott's late husband. If old Carl's shade really was lurking around here somewhere, Helen Alvarez would just have to get herself another detective.

I don't do ghosts. I definitely do not do ghosts.

3

Helen Alvarez and I left Mrs. Abbott in her Boston rocker and went to have a look around the premises. Starting with the rear porch.

A close-up examination of the back door revealed no marks on the locking plate or any other indication of forced entry. But the lock itself was of the unsafe push-button variety: anybody with half an ounce of ingenuity and a minimum of strength could pop it open in less than a minute. The cat's three bowls—water, dry food, wet food—were over next to the washer and dryer, ten feet from the door. Easy enough for someone to slip in here late at night, dose one of the bowls with poison, and slip out again after resetting the lock button.

From there Mrs. Alvarez and I went out into the rear yard. It was a cloudy day, with a biting wind off the Pacific—the kind of March day that made you wonder how much longer winter was going to hang around before spring finally kicked it out. The daffodils and some other flowers in narrow beds that ringed a small patch of lawn didn't know spring was a slow arrival this year; they gave the yard some color under the gloomy sky. The beds and the lawn were neatly kept—Mrs.

Alvarez's brother Leonard's doing, now that age and frail health had forced Margaret Abbott to give up gardening.

The yard itself was enclosed by fences, no gate in any of them; neighboring houses crowded in close on both flanks. But beyond the back fence, which was less than six feet high and easily climbable, was a kids' playground. I went across the lawn, around on the north side of the house, and found another trespasser's delight: a brick path that was open all the way to the street.

I walked down the path a ways, looking at the side wall of the house. Helen Alvarez and her brother had done a good job of eradicating the words that had been spray-painted there, except for the shadow of a *bullsh* that was half-hidden behind a privet hedge.

In the adjacent yard on that side, a man in a sweatshirt had been sweeping up blown leaves that had collected around what looked like a fruit tree in the center of a winter brown lawn. He'd stopped when he saw Mrs. Alvarez and me, stood leaning on his rake for a few seconds; now he came over to the fence, carrying the rake vertically in his right hand as if bearing a standard. He was about fifty, thin, balding, long jawed. He nodded to me, said to Mrs. Alvarez, "How's Margaret holding up?"

"Fair, Ev, just fair. She's got it into her head that a ghost, of all things, might be responsible."

"Ghost?"

"Her late husband come back to haunt her."

"Uh-oh. Sounds like she's ready to be put away for safe-keeping."

"Not yet she isn't. Not if this man"—Mrs. Alvarez patted my arm—"and I have anything to say about it. He's a detective and he is going to put a stop to what's been going on."

The neighbor gave me a speculative look. "Police?"

"Private investigator."

"Is that right?"

"Yes, and I hired him," Mrs. Alvarez said.

"To do what, exactly?"

"I told you—put a stop to what's been going on."

She introduced us. The thin guy's name was Everett Belasco.

He asked me, "So how're you gonna do it? You got ways that the police haven't?"

People always want to know how a private detective works. They think there is some special methodology that sets us apart from the police and even further apart from those in other public-service professions. Another by-product of half a century of fiction, films, and TV shows.

I told Belasco the truth. "No, I don't have any special methods. Just hard work and perseverance, with maybe a little luck thrown in." And of course it disappointed him, as it usually does.

"Well, you ask me," he said, "it's either bums or street punks."

"Bums?"

"City calls 'em homeless; I call 'em bums. Drug addicts, most of 'em, live like pigs over in Golden Gate Park. Panhandle, steal, leave dirty needles lying around, destroy property all over the damn place."

My opinion of Everett Belasco dropped a couple of notches. "Most of the encampments have been cleaned out," I said.

"Yeah, but not all of 'em. Every day I see some bum wandering around, relieving himself right out in plain sight. Punk kids, too, Mexicans, blacks. Gangs of 'em on weekends at Ocean Beach."

"What reason would kids or homeless people have to vandalize private property in this neighborhood?"

"They need a reason nowadays?"

"Any particular individuals you have in mind?"

"Nah. But I'll tell you this—the neighborhood's not safe like it used to be." He waggled the rake to emphasize his judgment. "Whole damn city's going to hell, you ask me."

I quit paying attention to him, asked Mrs. Alvarez if there had been any other cases of malicious mischief in the neighborhood recently.

"Not that I know about."

"So Margaret's the first," Belasco said. "They start with one person, an old lady can't defend herself; then they move on to somebody else. Me, for instance. Or you, Helen." He shook his head. "I'm telling you, it's either bums from the park or street punks."

As Mrs. Alvarez and I went on out front, I wondered if it would be worth running two or three late-night stakeouts on the Abbott home. Not me—Alex Chavez. I hate stakeouts of any kind; he doesn't mind them. If the harassment pattern held, there was liable to be another incident fairly soon. Worthwhile, then?

No. Not with two easy ways to get onto the property, front and back. One man couldn't watch them both, and on a pro bono case like this one, the expense of hiring a second part-time operative was prohibitive. Of course Chavez could run the stakeout alone from inside Mrs. Abbott's house, but that wouldn't do much good if the perp did his dirty work outside. If the situation posed a potential threat to Margaret Abbott's safety, a single or double stakeout would be warranted and hang the cost, but I didn't see it happening that way. All the mischief had been petty and none of it directed against

Mrs. Abbott personally. If there was another incident, it would follow the same pattern as the previous ones.

Belasco's insistence that homeless people or kids were responsible was misdirected venom and bigotry. It was true enough that the city was infested with aggressive panhandlers, chronic drunks and drug users who used the streets and parks as public toilets and sometimes destroyed both public and private property. And gang activity was rampant in the Mission and Visitacion Valley and Bayview–Hunters Point districts. But both genuine and bogus homeless pretty much confined themselves to certain sections—Market Street downtown, the Haight, the inner Mission—and the black and Latino gangs committed their acts of violence on their own turf and mostly against one another. Even those Belasco called street punks tended to be territorial, and their acts of vandalism were generally limited to spreading graffiti and breaking into parked cars.

The kind of malicious mischief Mrs. Abbott had been subjected to didn't have the feel or methodology of homeless, gang, or teenage troublemaking. No, it figured to be calculated to a specific purpose. Find that purpose and I'd find the person or persons responsible.

Helen Alvarez lived half a block to the west, just off Ulloa. This was a former blue-collar neighborhood, built in the thirties on what had once been windswept stretches of sand dunes. The parcels were small, the houses of mixed architectural styles and detached from one another, unlike the unesthetic shoulder-to-shoulder Dolger row houses farther inland. Built cheap, and bought cheap fifty years ago, but now worth small fortunes thanks to San Francisco's overinflated real estate market and a steady influx of Asian families, both American and foreign born, with money to spend and a desire for a piece of the city. Long time owners like Margaret Abbott and people who had lived here for decades like Helen Alvarez were now the exceptions rather than the rule.

The Alvarez house was of stucco and similar in type and size, if not in color, to the one owned by Mrs. Abbott. It was painted a toasty brown with orange-yellow trim, a combination that made me think of a huge and artfully constructed grilled-cheese sandwich. The garage door was up and a slope-shouldered man wearing a Giants baseball cap was doing something at a workbench inside. Helen Alvarez ushered me in that way.

The slope-shouldered man was Leonard Crenshaw. A few years older than his sister and on the dour side, he had lived here with her since the death of her husband eight years ago. Leonard had offered to move in, she'd told me, to help out with chores and to keep her from being lonely. If he had a profession or a job, she hadn't confided what it was.

"Don't mind saying," he said to me, "I think Helen made a mistake shelling out money to hire you."

I didn't tell him that I was working pro bono; neither did she. "Why is that, Mr. Crenshaw?" I asked.

"Always sticking her nose in other people's business. Been like that her whole life. Nosy and bossy."

"Better than putting my head in the sand like an ostrich," Mrs. Alvarez said. She didn't seem upset or annoyed by her brother's remarks. I had the impression this was an old verbal tug-of-war between siblings, one that went back a lot of years through a lot of different incidents.

"Can't just live her life and let others live theirs," Crenshaw said. "It's Charley Doyle should be taking care of his aunt and her problems, spending his money on expensive detectives."

Expensive detectives, I thought. Leonard, if you only knew what some of the big agencies charge for their services. And how seldom they work pro bono, or take on cases like this one.

"Charley Doyle can barely take care of himself," she said. "He has two brain cells and one of them is usually passed out drunk. All he cares about is gambling and liquor and cheap women."

"A heavy gambler, is he?" I asked.

"Oh, I don't think so. He's too lazy and too stupid. Besides, he plays poker with Ev Belasco and Ev is so tight he squeaks."

Crenshaw said, "You know what's going to happen to you, Helen, talking about people behind their backs that way. You'll spend eternity hanging by your tongue, that's what."

"Better than spending eternity hanging by what you've been overusing all your adult life."

"Funny. You're a riot, you are."

"Oh, put a sock in it, Leonard."

He didn't put a sock in it. He said grumpily, "Telling tales about people, hiring detectives, sticking your nose in where it doesn't belong. Next thing you know, *our* phone'll start ringing in the middle of the night, somebody'll bust one of *our* windows."

"Nonsense."

"Is it? Stir things up, you're bound to make 'em worse. For everybody. You mark my words."

Helen Alvarez and I went upstairs, into a cluttered living room, and she provided me with contact addresses for Charley Doyle and the address of the real estate agency owned by the Pattersons.

"Don't mind Leonard," she said then. "He's not such a curmudgeon as he pretends to be. This crazy business with Margaret has him almost as upset as it has me."

"I try not to be judgmental, Mrs. Alvarez."

"So do I," she said. "Now you go give those Pattersons hell, you hear? A taste of their own medicine, the dirty swine."

I didn't go give the Pattersons hell or anything else, including the benefit of the doubt. Tomorrow was soon enough for that. It was late afternoon now, the end of my workday, and what I wanted was a hot shower, a cold beer, and a quiet dinner, in that order.

So I went home.

And walked straight into a sudden family crisis.

4

JAKE RUNYON

"Jumpers," Abe Melikian said sourly. "God, I hate 'em, I hate 'em with a passion. They want to jump, why don't they go jump off a bridge, jump off a building? No, they got to jump on my poor ass instead."

Runyon made a sympathetic noise.

"As if I don't have enough troubles," Melikian said. "I got a bad back, I got hemorrhoids, and now my doctor says I got to have a hip replacement. I'm falling apart here. Business is lousy, and now I got another jumper trying to screw me. This Troy Madison bum loses himself down a sewer hole with the rest of the goddamn rats I'm out thirty-one point five K, and I can't afford the loss. You understand what I'm saying to you?"

Bill had worked a few bail-jump cases for Melikian in the past and had warned Runyon he was a chronic complainer and poor-mouth. In fact, he now owned one of the more successful bail bonds outfits in the city: half a dozen employees and offices right across Bryant Street from the Hall of Justice. Healthy as a horse, too, Bill said, in spite of his usual litany of physical complaints. Right. Robust, fit-looking man in his late fifties, with a full head of dark brown hair that didn't look dyed.

Runyon said, "I understand. You want him found as fast as possible."

"Fast, that's right. Before he disappears so nobody can find him."

"What time was his court appearance this morning?"

"Ten o'clock. Soon as I found out he didn't show, I sent one of my people over to his apartment. Gone. Flew the coop last night."

"How do you know it was last night?"

"One of the neighbors saw him leave. Him and that skanky broad he lives with. Carrying suitcases, both of 'em."

"What's the neighbor's name?"

"I don't know; ask Frank outside. He's the one talked to her."

"The neighbor have any idea where they were headed?"

"Hell no," Melikian said. "Jumpers, they're like mimes— they don't say a word to nobody."

"What about Madison's lawyer?"

"Public defender. Surprised Madison jumped, he said. Met with him two days ago, Madison promised he'd show, that was good enough for the PD. Why's everybody frigging incompetent these days?"

"Everybody isn't."

"Meaning you? Better not be. I don't know you, but I know your boss; he's plenty competent. How come he didn't come himself? He can't be bothered with Abe Melikian anymore?"

"He's semiretired. I do most of the fieldwork for the agency now."

"Yeah? So I guess you must be okay. I'd hate to have to call in a bounty hunter. Those buggers want fifteen, twenty percent of the bond—I can't afford to pay fees like that, put me straight out of business."

Runyon said, "Tell me about Madison."

"Tell you what? It's all in that file you got there in your hand."

"I'd rather hear it from you first."

Melikian screwed up his face until it resembled a mournful hound's. "A doper," he said. "You can't trust dopers, they're the dregs, they're gene-pool scum. Even the first-timers, and he's not a first-timer—he was busted three times before this last one."

"All for possession with intent to sell?"

"No. Just this last time for dealing."

"Jump bail before?"

"No. You think I'd've put up his bond if he had? Ahh, why the hell'd he have to pick on me this time? I should've turned him and that brother of his down flat; that's what I should've done."

"Why didn't you?"

"Why. The man asks why. I got mouths to feed and bills and salaries to pay, that's why. I got to have a hip replacement operation, I already told you that. So what choice do I have but to serve the dregs, the scum, unless my shit detector tells me don't do it. Only it wasn't working with this Madison pair. The doper came across all contrite and respectful and I fell for it like he was my first client ever. Maybe my shit detector's busted permanently along with everything else I got wrong with me. I tell you, I'm falling apart here."

Runyon said, "His brother put up your fee. Coy Madison, is it?"

"Yeah. Coy. Coy and Troy. Some names."

"What'd Coy say when you told him his brother didn't show?

"He was pissed, what else? He's out thirty-five hundred, or his wife is."

"The wife's money?"

"Yeah," Melikian said. "He works in some art supply store, doesn't earn much of his own."

"Either of them have any idea where his brother might be?"

"He says no."

"Or why Troy jumped bail?"

"Why? Why do you think? Figured he'd be convicted, didn't want to do the time. Goddamn jumpers are all alike."

"He have any other relatives?"

"No."

"What about friends?"

"Dopers like that, they don't have friends, they just have customers."

"He's got at least one," Runyon said.

"Yeah? Who?"

"The woman he lives with."

Melikian managed to half-curl his upper lip. "Her. What the jumper sees in her I can't imagine, unless she does something fancy in bed. Looks like she's been dragged a few times behind a Muni bus. Older than him, must be thirty-five."

"What's her name?"

"Jennifer Piper. Another doper. She got caught in the same bust, but the cops didn't hold her. Not enough evidence she was dealing, too."

"Where've they been living?"

"Apartment on Valencia. Address is in the file." Melikian's

voice was edged with impatience now. "Everything else you need is in the file. So how about you get moving instead of sitting here asking me questions, find that goddamn jumper so I don't lose my thirty-one point five K."

"I'll do my best."

"I don't want to hear do your best. You think my doctor's gonna give me a hip replacement I tell him I'll do my best to pay him for it? Results, that's what I want. That damn jumper back in jail where he belongs, that's what I want."

Runyon had nothing to say to that. He'd learned long ago that you didn't argue with clients or respond to less than reasonable demands from the aggressive ones like Melikian. You just nodded, said you'd be in touch. And went away to do exactly what you'd said you would—your best, always.

In his car he went through the printout of the Madison file. There were two pics of Troy Madison in addition to the usual bio sheet, one the booking photo from his latest arrest, the other a head-and-shoulders snap probably taken by one of Melikian's employees. Skinny kid at five ten, 160 pounds. Long reddish hair, scraggly beard, pockmarked cheeks—not much to look at, but memorable enough once you'd seen him. Runyon slipped both photos into his jacket pocket.

The two brothers had been born in Bakersfield, Troy the younger by two years—twenty-eight now. Both parents deceased and no living relatives except an eighty-five-year-old grandmother in a Visalia nursing home. Never married. Mechanic by trade, also worked as a truck driver. Current address: 244 Valencia Street. Arrested four times on narcotics charges over the past seven years, all in San Francisco—three for possession of methamphetamines and crack cocaine, the recent intent-to-sell bust made outside a Mission District nightclub by two undercover narcs. The possession charges had resulted in a couple of slaps on the wrist and one six-month stay in the county jail; the current bust involved sufficient amounts of meth and crack to land him in Folsom if he was convicted. Melikian's shit detector had malfuctioned where Madison was concerned, all right. Prime jumper candidate from the get-go.

Madison's brother, Coy, and his wife lived on 19th Street. He was manager of Noe Valley Arts & Crafts Supply on 24th; Arletta Madison was a self-employed sculptress, either one of the few successful artists of that type or she had money of her own that her husband wasn't privy to without permission.

There was nothing in the file on Jennifer Piper.

Runyon called the agency, asked Tamara to run checks on the Madison brothers, Piper, and Arletta Madison and to find out if she could turn up any individuals with ties, particularly criminal ties, to Troy Madison. Then he got rolling.

The apartment building where Madison and Piper had been living was an old four-story stucco pile with a buff-colored façade, a couple of blocks off Market. The lobby mailbox that bore Madison's name but not Jennifer Piper's was 3B. Runyon rang the bell three times, just making sure, before he looked up the building manager, a fat woman with hair the color of Cheez Whiz. She had nothing to tell him. "I don't pay no attention to what the other tenants do unless they don't pay their rent on time," she said. "Troy Madison pays his on time, that's all I know, that's all I want to know."

Runyon went back into the vestibule and thumbed the bell on the box marked *Adams,* the name of the woman who'd seen Madison and Piper leaving with their suitcases. No answer. He rang the other bells one at a time, got three responses. One of the three wouldn't talk to him; the other two were willing enough, if hardly a font of information.

"I heard Madison got arrested for selling drugs," one of them said, "but he never tried to push any around here. I'd've turned him in if he had. I don't have nothing to do with drugs, mister. One of my sister's kids died of a heroin overdose three years ago."

"The Piper woman?" the other neighbor said. "Sure, I seen her around. Unfriendly as hell. Stare right through you like you were a piece of glass. No, I don't know where she works. Don't work anywhere, for all I know. I seen her around here all hours, day and night."

So much for Valencia Street, at least for the time being. Next stop: Noe Valley.

He wondered what Bryn was doing right now.

Funny how thoughts like that popped into his head lately. He'd be thinking about something else or not thinking about anything, driving someplace or no place, and then all of a sudden she'd be there in his mind. Just the way Colleen had been in the twenty good years before the cancer diagnosis. Happened all the time then, not just occasionally, but he'd been deeply in love with Colleen—the love of his life. He wasn't in love with Bryn. Or was he? Maybe, a little . . . more than a little. But not in the same way, now or ever.

With Colleen the connection had been so complete that when the cancer had finally destroyed her, it'd nearly destroyed him, too. With Bryn it was different. A closeness built on friendship, understanding, a gradually hardening bond of trust. Gentle intimacy, even in bed the past month. Two damaged people, her by the stroke that had paralyzed one side of her face, him by Colleen's lingering death and the black hole it had left inside him. Leaning on each other for support, sure, but it was more than that—it was helping each other learn how to feel again, how to care about themselves again.

She'd be working now, he thought, as she did most afternoons. Maybe on one of her watercolors or charcoal sketches, maybe on the computer-generated graphic designs that paid her bills. She'd refused spousal support when her cold, selfish ex-husband divorced her after the stroke. Too proud, too self-sufficient. She'd even insisted on paying a share of the support for her only kid, nine-year-old Robert Jr., Bobby.

Bobby had spent this past weekend with her—one of the two weekends a month she was allowed to have her son to herself. The ex-husband, the kind of lawyer that gave the profession a bad name, had manipulated it that way. Made some sort of arrangement with a family court judge who granted him full custody except for the monthly weekend visits and one week in the summer, the decision based on the lie that Bryn's stroke and disfigurement made her less than fit to raise the boy as a single mom. Bastards. And now Robert Sr. was getting married again, which meant a new "mother" for Bobby, an increased feeling of alienation for Bryn.

Nothing she could do about it. Nothing Runyon could, either, except be there for her when she needed him—particularly during one of her periodic bouts of near-suicidal depression. He'd been suicidal himself after Colleen died, come close more than once to eating his gun; he knew all about the waves of black melancholy and the death-wish impulses. He'd fought them, beat them off, finally buried them. Bryn would do the same with his help and support. He believed that and he felt that she was starting to believe it, too.

He hoped the weekend had gone well. He hadn't talked to her since Thursday night, didn't feel it was right to intrude on her private time with her son. Had she taken his advice to be more affectionate with the boy? So afraid Bobby would pull away from her because of her deformity that she'd let an uncomfortable distance build up between them, not once in his presence removing the scarf she wore constantly over the frozen side of her face.

That wouldn't change, at least not for some time. She still wouldn't let Runyon see her without the scarf, or touch her face or kiss her. Sex in the dark, bodies close but heads apart at awkward angles.

Hurt and lonely, both of them. It was what had drawn them together, what would keep them together until something happened to end their relationship or make it permanent.

Better not think about that now. Carpe diem. It had been so long since he'd felt like seizing any day, looked forward to something other than filling up the long empty hours with work and aimless driving. Enjoy it while it lasted. Be grateful for the chance to feel alive again.

Noe Valley, between the east side of Twin Peaks and the Mission District, was one of the city's thriving upscale neighborhoods. Fashionable older homes and apartment buildings, and along 24th Street blocks of restaurants, coffeehouses, bookstores, taverns, small businesses. Parking was at a premium; it took Runyon ten minutes to find a space within a block and a half of 24th and Castro, where Noe Valley Arts & Crafts was located.

Small place: long, narrow, with shelves and displays along

the walls, more shelving down the middle, and an upfront counter. The girl behind the counter was eighteen or nineteen, gold rings and studs in her ears, nose, and upper lip, and fingernails painted the color of a ripe eggplant. The stud in her lip sparkled when she told him, smiling, that Mr. Madison was in his office in back. She offered to go fetch him, but Runyon said he'd just go on back, he had some personal business to discuss.

The office door was open, revealing a small, tidy office and the man standing at an old-fashioned file cabinet along one wall. He was taller than his brother, a couple of inches over six feet, and also red haired, but with the kind of smooth baby-skin face that would sprout only enough whiskers for twice-weekly shaves. A weak chin and close-set eyes kept him from being good-looking. He glanced around, blinking, as Runyon stepped into the doorway.

"This is a private office," Madison said. "The girl at the counter can get you anything you need—"

"Afraid not, Mr. Madison." Runyon introduced himself, showed his license. "I'm here about your brother."

Madison said, "Oh, God," in a voice that was half-pained, half-irritated. "Come in; shut the door." Then, when Runyon had complied, "I suppose that bondsman, Melikian, hired you to find Troy."

"My agency. That's right."

"Well, I don't have any idea where he went." Madison moved away from the file cabinet, around behind his desk. Most men of his height had an easy way of walking, but his movements were awkward and loose-jointed, almost a duck waddle. "A long damn way from here, I hope. So far away you never find him."

"If you feel that way, why did you arrange for his bail?"

"You don't know him," Madison said. "Nobody knows him like I do."

"Meaning?"

"He puts on a good act, pretends to be easygoing, everybody's friend. But inside he's just the opposite. A mean, violent son of a bitch. He used to beat me up when we were kids, just for the hell of it. I took more abuse from him than anybody else in my life, including my wife."

"He threatened you, is that it?"

"Not at first. Claimed he was innocent, that he'd been set up and could prove it at his trial. Swore he'd pay the money back as soon as he could—a crock; he never paid anybody back a dime in his life. I told him no, we couldn't afford it. That's when he turned ugly. He knew we had the money. Said he'd hurt me, hurt Arletta, if we didn't bail him out."

"You could've ignored the threats, left him in jail."

"Sure. Maybe he'd've been convicted and maybe he wouldn't, and even if he was he'd spend, what, a couple of years in prison. What do you think he'd do when he got out? No, you just don't know him and what he's capable of."

"Did you expect him to jump bail?"

"I thought he might. He was in jail for six months a few years ago; you probably know that. He hated it, hated the idea of going to prison."

"So you were hoping he would jump, go on the run."

"Well, what if I was? I didn't help him do it, did I?"

Same as. But Runyon didn't put the thought into words.

"I have a right to protect myself and my wife," Madison said defensively. "The best way I can."

"She agree?"

"Sure she agrees. Why ask that?"

"I understand it was her money that paid Melikian."

"Her money." Madison's mouth thinned down even more, until his smooth baby face seemed lipless. "Christ, I get tired of hearing that. So she's gotten lucky with those sculptures of hers, darling of the critics and gallery owners, so what? We're married, it's *my* money, too."

Runyon said mildly, "Abe Melikian says you had to ask her for the thirty-five hundred. Prenup?"

Anger kindled in Madison's pale blue eyes. "That's none of your business. My personal affairs have nothing to do with my brother skipping out on his bail."

Runyon let it go. "When did you last see him?"

"The day he got bailed out."

"No contact with him since? No demands for more money?"

"No. At least not yet."

"Then he might have some of his own stashed away. Or a supply of drugs or a source to get him some that he can turn into ready cash. Any idea who his suppliers are?"

"No."

"His friends?"

"No. They're all drug freaks like that bitch he lives with. I don't have anything to do with people like that."

"But you do know her. Jennifer Piper."

"Not before he was arrested. I hardly ever saw Troy, except when he needed money. She was at the jail when I went to see him. Christ, what a piece she is. Tattoos, greasy hair, body like a scarecrow. She gave me the creeps."

Runyon asked, "He still have ties to anyone in Bakersfield?"

"Not that I know about. He wouldn't've gone back there,

if that's what you're thinking. He hated growing up there; we both did."

"What do you think, then, Mr. Madison? Is he running or hiding out somewhere locally?"

"I can't answer that. Troy's not smart; he's just cunning—and so messed up on drugs there's no telling what he might do."

Runyon laid one of his business cards on the desk. "Let me know if he contacts you for any reason."

"I don't think so," Madison said. "I help you catch him and he finds out, Arletta and I will be the ones to suffer when he gets out of prison. I hope to Christ none of us ever sees his ugly face again."

5

TAMARA

Vonda's brother James was a partner in a construction company called Three Brothers. Specialized in home repair for black home owners and landlords in Bayview–Hunters Point, the Fillmore, and other parts of the city. In the last couple of years Three Brothers Construction had expanded their operation, moved to a bigger location, and started bidding on small developments of new houses both inside and outside the city. James was the smartest of the three, the driving force behind the expansion. Natural-born hustler and promoter, so he ran the white-collar end of the business while his two partners did the blue-collar work.

Back in his high school days in Redwood City, James had run with a bunch of local gangbangers hooked in with an even tougher crowd in East Palo Alto. Got into heavy stuff for a while—drugs, using and selling both, and Tamara had heard rumors of weapons dealing and strong-arm robberies. What had straightened him up was watching a shotgun blast blow off most of his best friend's face during a drug deal gone sour. Standing right next to the dude when it went down, took some of the blast himself and spent a week in the hospital. There hadn't been enough evidence to charge him with anything, so he came out free and clear—with a whole new attitude. Changed his life around. Found some new, nonviolent friends to hang with, got himself a construction job, learned the trade, then hooked up with his two partners and started Three Brothers Construction with a loan from a minority small-business packager.

Funny how things turned out sometimes. Good and bad both. Tamara and Vonda had both been pretty wild themselves, chasing with some rough homies, experimenting with weed and sex, all cornrowed and grunge dressed and party ready. Done the racist thing, too, hating and cussing the white man's world same as James did. And now here they were ten years later, all three of them living in San Francisco and holding down jobs they would've sneered at in their bad-ass days. Tamara partnered with a white man in a detective agency, Vonda a sales rep at the S.F. Design Center, James a damn-near executive in a successful construction outfit. Solid members of the establishment they'd once scorned—a world that still belonged to the white man but that had opened up and changed and was still changing. Any damn thing was possible for an African American or any other minority now. A half-black man being elected president proved that.

Tamara and Vonda had shed the racist bullshit, learned how to get along with people of any color or no color. Not James. He'd escaped the gang jungle and built a good life for himself, but when it came to white folks, the best he'd learned to do was tolerate them. Went off like a rocket when Vonda announced she was pregnant and going to marry Ben Sherman, who was not only white but Jewish besides. Showed up at Ben's apartment on Tel Hill and got right in his face and tried to warn him off. No way that was gonna happen, a real love match there between those two. Ben had been cool and stayed cool with James. Made a real effort to turn him around. Hadn't worked, but Ben had gotten further than any other white guy had. James still didn't approve of the marriage, but he'd shaken Ben's hand at the wedding and toasted him with a glass of champagne at the reception.

James had had a thing for Tamara in their bad-ass days, but she hadn't given him any encouragement. Just not her type. He still resented her for the rejection, and the fact that she'd gone into the investigation business hadn't made him like her any better. She was fuzz to him, not much different from her old man—a detective on the Redwood City PD who'd given James and his gangbangers plenty of grief. Sellouts, the way he saw the Corbins. Oppressors of their own people. And nothing she or Vonda or anybody else said or did was ever likely to change his mind.

So she had to be as cool with James as Ben had been. Not let him goad her into losing her temper. Last time she'd seen him was at the wedding and reception, and he hadn't said ten words to her that day. Looked right through her most of the time. Well, this wasn't a social event; this was business—important business. She was a professional, and professionals could get information out of anybody if they handled it right.

Three Brothers Construction's new home was on Industrial Street, near the 280 and 101 freeway interchange. Tamara closed up the agency early and drove over there, calling first to make sure James would be in. But she didn't make an appointment or give her name, just told the woman who answered that she was a friend. If James knew she was coming, be just like him to refuse to see her or duck out early himself.

She'd never been to the new place before and she had to admit it was steps up from the old one on 3rd in Hunters Point. Offices at one end of a big warehouse that the brothers had renovated themselves, and an equipment and storage yard that took up half a block. Fifteen full-time employees and twenty more part-timers, plus a handful of subcontractors on the bigger jobs. Mr. James McGee, contractor. Mr. James McGee, capitalist. She'd never have believed it possible, down in Redwood City. Neither would Vonda. And Pop least of all. He'd figured James would end up dead or in prison like so many others.

The business offices were plain and functional; so was Nancy, the office manager. Tamara said she was the friend who'd called and if James wasn't busy, she'd just go on into his private office and surprise him. He wasn't busy and Nancy didn't offer any objections, so in she walked.

James was behind a big messy desk with a batch of blueprints spread out in front of him. He glanced up, then fixed her with a long scowly stare. "Shit," he said.

"Good to see you, too."

"I got no time for you. Or any other Oreo."

"I'm no more white inside than you are."

"Partner's a white man, isn't he? Clients mostly white?"

"None of your disrespect, okay? You work for whites yourself."

"The hell I do."

"The hell you don't. Who you think runs the Franchise Tax Board in Sacramento, the IRS in Washington? Black men?"

Right thing to say. It wiped away the glare and brought a wry little chuckle out of him. He leaned back in his chair, clasped his hands behind his head. Handsome dude, she had to admit, much better looking than he'd been in his grunge days. Lean and mean, thick beard trimmed short, skin smooth as brown silk. Those bushy-browed black eyes had once burned like fire; the heat was still there, but the fire had been banked by time and success. He cleaned up pretty well, too. She remembered his wedding outfit: pin-striped charcoal suit, saffron-colored shirt, pink tie. Dressed more conservatively here on the job—tan sports jacket, open-necked blue shirt—and none of it showed a wrinkle or rumple. No question the new James was a big improvement on the old one.

He said, "So what the hell you doing here?"

"Vonda didn't tell you about me and Lucas Zeller?"

"We don't talk much since she married her white Jew."

"Yeah, well, Lucas and I had a thing a couple of weeks ago."

"Uh-huh." James scratched one long finger through his beard, looking at her narrow eyed. "Why'd you hook up with that ugly dude anyway? You that hard up for a man?"

Tamara said between her teeth, "Wasn't nobody else asking."

"No surprise there." But his eyes were on her body, roaming. "Lost some fat around your middle, looks like."

"That's right."

"Stand to lose some more."

She bit off a sharp comeback, said instead, "You're not exactly buff yourself, my man."

"I'm not your man, and damn glad of it." Lopsided grin. "You may be hard up, but I'm not. Saw the fox I was with at the wedding, right? She gives me all the lovin' I can handle."

Fox? "Cat" was a better word—sleek black cat with claws

and a big red tongue in a big red mouth. "I'll bet she does," Tamara said.

"So what you want from me?"

"I'm looking for him."

"Who? Zeller?"

"His name's not Zeller."

"No? Well, I could give a shit less."

"I know that."

"Then what you doing here, bugging me?"

"Answers to a few questions, James, that's all I want."

"Yeah? What'd you ever do for me?"

"Been a good friend to Vonda, helped her out a couple of times when she needed it. How about that?"

Now the scowl was back. But then he said, "What'd the dude do, throw you over for some guy?"

"No."

"Vonda tell you he's on the down low?"

"You know she did."

"He give you a disease?"

"No. I had myself tested."

"So?"

"The man's more than just on the down low," Tamara said. "He's a thief and maybe worse. Stole the real Lucas Zeller's briefcase, wallet, identity, and some cash from his checking account. Stole his identity."

James took that in, not saying anything. The look he gave her then was a little less hostile. "You sure about all that?"

"I'm sure."

"Well, you know that much, how come you can't find him? Hot-shit de-tective like you."

"Not enough information yet."

"Who you working for, the real Zeller?"

"No. For myself."

"Uh-huh, I get it. The woman-scorned bit."

"Let's cut out the bullshit, James, all right? I need some help and I'm not ashamed to ask for it. Even from you. You gonna talk straight to me or you just gonna go on dissing me?"

For a few seconds she thought she'd pushed him too hard, that he'd go off on her and chase her out. But he didn't. Stared at her for half a minute, then let loose a grunting sound, leaned back in his chair, and said, "All right, sweet cheeks, do your thing. But don't take too long. I got work to do."

Sweet cheeks. She hated that name, even more than she hated Pop calling her Sweetness, and James knew it. But she knew better than to call him on it. Stay cool, Tamara.

"Where'd you meet him?" she asked. "Some sort of event at Moscone Center, wasn't it?"

"Yeah. Sports memorabilia show."

James was into sports in a big way. Football, basketball, baseball, golf . . . you name it, he followed it, and sometimes bet on games and matches. Liked rubbing elbows with black players for local teams, current and retired, and not just out of hero worship. Business reasons, too. He was always looking to connect with somebody who might do him and Three Brothers Construction some good.

"So what happened?" she asked. "He approach you or the other way around?"

"He did. Real friendly. Too fuckin' friendly."

"But you didn't figure it that way at first."

James didn't say anything. His silence was answer enough.

"He say what his business was?"

"Investments."

"That's all? Just investments?"

"That's all."

"Try to hustle you?"

"No."

"Say anything about the sports club he wanted you to join?"

"Not then. But that friend of his brought it up."

Tamara jumped on that. "Friend? What friend?"

"Dude that brought him to the show." The scowl darkened. "I should've known they were queers right then. Little guy kept giving me looks like I was a hunk of raw meat and he was a junkyard dog."

"What was his name?"

"Hell, I don't remember."

"Come on, James; it's important. Think about it, try to remember."

". . . Easy."

"What's easy?"

"Told me to call him Doctor Easy, everybody did."

"He didn't give you his real name?"

"Dawkins, Hawkins, something like that."

"Doctor Easy Dawkins? Doesn't sound right— Wait. Initials? E.Z.?"

"Whatever."

"You remember what kind of doctor?"

"One of those spine snappers."

"Chiropractor? Here in the city?"

Shrug. "Gave me a business card, but I didn't look at it."

"You still have it?"

"Threw it away on my way out."

"I don't suppose Zeller had a business card?"

"No. Asked for one of mine and I gave it to him. Didn't see any reason not to."

Tamara asked, "What'd they tell you about the club?"

"Brought it up real casual. Said they were big sports fans, got together once or twice a month with some other guys to kick back, have a few drinks, watch videos and films. Five of them now, was I interested in being number six?"

"And you said?"

"No. Fan clubs ain't my thing."

"So then what happened with Zeller? After the sports show, I mean."

"Christ, woman, how many questions you gonna ask? I told you, I got work to do."

"Just a few more. Zeller call you up or what?"

"Or what. Showed up here a couple days later. Walked right in without an appointment, same as you did."

Scoping out the place, she thought, to get an idea of how much James was worth.

"Said he was in the neighborhood, thought he'd stop by. Said he'd enjoyed meeting me at the show, figured maybe we could have a few drinks, get to know each other better. Tried to get me to change my mind about joining that goddamn club."

"Hint around that it was a switch-hitters thing?"

"Not that time," James said. "I told him I still wasn't interested. He didn't push it and I figured that was the end of it. And then bam, next week he shows up at the wedding reception."

"How'd he know about it?"

"I don't know, saw Nancy's invitation, maybe—she had it on her desk. Dude's got more balls than a basketball team, showing up the way he did, claiming I invited him. I never saw him come in. Must've been there awhile before I spotted him and threw him out."

"Saw him one more time, right?"

"Couple of days later. Showed up here again like nothing ever happened. Walked right in—Nancy was out to lunch."

"One last try to hook you into the club."

"Yeah." Some of the old fierce burn had come into James's eyes. "Invited me to a meeting that weekend. Said the other guys were professional people or businessmen, all married men and none of 'em judgmental. Then he laughed like something was funny. Said, well, except one man who was but wouldn't be."

"Was but wouldn't be what? Judgmental?"

"Fuckin' double-talk."

"*All* married men? Including himself?"

"What he said."

"Give you any of their names?"

"No."

"Tell you where the meeting was?"

"SoMa loft belongs to one of 'em. Said we'd watch some rare Super Bowl film one of 'em had, have a few drinks, have a good time—maybe experiment if we felt like it, but only one-on-one and strictly in private. All very discreet. That was the word he used, 'discreet.' We were standing over there by the door and he starts telling me all this and leaning up close, putting his hand on my arm and looking at me the way the little bugger did at the show. Plain as hell then where he was coming from."

"You accuse him of being on the down low?"

"Damn right. Him and his buddies. He just shrugged, said

did it matter if they were? I told him yeah, damn straight it mattered, and then I threw his ass out. I should've busted his head for him."

"Too bad you didn't."

"You know the last thing the fucker said? Said he guessed he'd misread me. Misread me! All along he thought I was a switch-hitter like him!"

James had worked himself into a brooding rage by then, glowering all over his face. She wouldn't get anything more out of him—lucky she'd gotten as much as she had. She slipped on out of there herself before he started venting his rage on her. The way he was sitting, rigid, staring back into his bitter memory, he didn't even see her go.

6

When I came into the condo, Kerry was out on the balcony with the sliding glass door wide open. Ordinarily there wouldn't have been anything unusual in that. We live in Diamond Heights, on the side of one of San Francisco's seven hills, and on clear days and nights the balcony view is pretty alluring. But the day had turned even colder as night approached; the wind swirling in through the open door had an arctic bite. And she was standing out there at the railing with her hair tangled and streaming, arms folded, wearing nothing but a light sweater and skirt.

I went out to stand beside her. She looked my way, gave me a wan little smile. There was color in her face from the cold and her eyes were teary. Not from the wind; the unhappy expression in them said she'd been crying. That scared me. The first thing I thought of was her breast cancer, in remission now but always and forever a lingering fear.

"Hey," I said, "what're you doing out here?"

"Trying to decide what to do."

"About what?"

"I'm glad you're home," she said.

"Me, too. Do about what? Kerry, you haven't been to see your oncologist . . . ?"

"No, it's nothing like that."

"Cybil?" Her mother was eighty-seven and in failing health.

"No. Cybil's all right."

"Then what?"

She sighed and unfolded her arms. Extended one fisted hand in my direction to show me what was on her palm.

Rough-textured, bronze-colored tin box, about the size of the ones sore-throat lozenges come in, with the same kind of hinged lid. Plain, no markings except for a few scratches and dents.

"Open it," she said.

I flipped up the lid. Inside was a rectangle of cotton, and when I poked inside that I found a clear plastic tube, about three inches long, mostly full of a white powdery substance. I knew what the substance was even before I pulled the little cork stopper in one end of the tube, licked a finger, and tipped out enough for a bitter taste on the tip of my tongue.

Cocaine.

The relief I'd been feeling died in a sensation like an acid burn. "Where'd you get this?"

"I found it. A few minutes ago."

"Where?"

"In Emily's room."

"Oh, Christ, no."

"I went in to get my *Roget's*," Kerry said. "She was using it last night and I needed to look up a word. The box was on her desk, in plain sight, and when I picked up the thesaurus I accidentally knocked it off. It popped open when it hit the floor."

Emily. Sweet, smart, intelligent, forthright, straight-arrow

Emily. Not your typical rebellious thirteen-year-old; just the opposite, in fact. In the four years since Kerry and I had adopted her, she'd never given us any cause to distrust her. Not once.

I put the tube back into its cotton nest, closed the tin box, and slipped it into my coat pocket. "Come on," I said, "let's go inside. It's freezing out here."

"Yes."

We went in and I shut the door. The living room was cold now, even though I could hear the furnace pumping warm air through the vents. I took Kerry's hands in mine, chafed them until I could feel some of the chill go away.

"Did you find anything else?"

"No. Just what's in the box."

"But you looked. Searched her room."

"You know I did. I had to, didn't I?"

"Sure you did. I would've done the same."

The privacy thing. We had a pact in this family: always respect one another's right to privacy. Even under the circumstances, Kerry felt guilty at breaking the pact. Was that what Emily had counted on, why she'd left the box on her desk in plain sight? Flaunting it because she felt safe? No, that wasn't like her. But hell, it wasn't like her to bring drugs home in the first place.

Kerry said, "I keep telling myself it's not as bad as it looks. That there must be some innocent explanation."

"Like what?"

"I don't know. Something. We had the drug talk with her, didn't we? Both of us?"

"Yeah, we had the drug talk."

"She swore she'd never have anything to do with drugs."

"She probably meant it at the time. But thirteen's a bad

age, you know that. And peer pressure can be more persuasive than parental pressure."

"But my God . . . pot's bad enough, but cocaine . . ." Kerry sank heavily into her chair. "Maybe she hasn't tried it yet. Maybe somebody gave it to her and she's just thinking about it."

"Maybe."

"But you don't think so."

"I don't know what to think. I'm as hammered by this as you are."

"It's after five. She should be home by now."

"Where'd she go after school?"

"The library to study with a couple of her friends. So she said."

"Don't start doubting her, babe."

"Aren't you doubting her? After this?"

"I'm trying to keep an open mind."

"So am I. Oh, God, I hate this—I fucking *hate* it!"

Kerry almost never used the *f* word. And hearing it from her didn't have any effect on me; I felt like using it myself. Neither of us had been this upset since the early stages of her breast cancer.

To calm both of us down, I went into the kitchen and poured her a glass of wine and opened the beer I'd been wanting for myself. The alcohol did its job, but there was no enjoyment in the after-work drink now. The beer seemed bitter, left a lingering sour aftertaste.

"When she gets home," Kerry said, "let me do the talking. You just back me up."

"Always," I said.

Emily came in fifteen minutes later. All breezy and bouncy as usual—until she saw Kerry and me in the living room, standing like a couple of stone statues. She stopped, her smile sliding away, and blinked her brown eyes and said, "What's the matter?"

Kerry told her, flat voiced, to take her coat off and then come back in and sit down.

"Why? What's going on?"

"Just do what I asked."

Emily looked at her, looked at me, bit a corner of her lip, and sidled off to hang up her coat. When she came back, Kerry and I were both sitting down again in our side-by-side chairs. Emily went around and perched on the couch with her knees together and her hands in her lap, her gaze on a neutral point between us.

She looked very young sitting there and at the same time almost grown-up: lipstick, eye shadow, a sweater too tight and a skirt too short for my liking. A real beauty in the making, the only worthwhile gift she'd gotten from her screwed-up birth parents. Those big brown eyes, creamy skin, delicate bone structure, long silky hair, a trim body that was already filling out noticeably. Heartbreaker someday. Males would swarm around her—probably had started to already, though she didn't talk much about boys. Or have any boyfriends yet, as far as Kerry and I knew.

They grow up so damn fast these days, I thought. Everybody says so—it's not just my perception. They're kids— Emily had been ten when she first came into our lives—and then all of a sudden they're virtual adults with adult attitudes, needs, vices. No transition period, or so it seemed. No time for an extended childhood and a slow easing into the grown-up world, as there had been with my generation. We hadn't been adults, hadn't considered ourselves adults, until seventeen or eighteen; nowadays kids stopped being kids as early as twelve. Or thirteen.

Nobody said anything for a minute or so. We all just sat there. Up to me to get this started because I had the tin box in my pocket. I took it out and set it on the coffee table between us, unopened.

Emily looked at it, closed her eyes, opened them again. "You've been in my room," she said. Not accusing, not sullen or angry—emotions she seldom expressed. She sounded hurt.

Kerry said, "I went to get my thesaurus. The box was right there on your desk."

"That's supposed to be my private space."

"I just told you—I wasn't snooping. How long have you been using drugs?"

"I *don't* use drugs. Never."

"Are you going to tell us you don't know what's in there?"

"I didn't, not at first."

"But now you do."

"It's cocaine, isn't it." Statement, not a question.

"And you've been thinking about trying it."

"No."

"Don't lie to us, Emily. The evidence is right there in front of you."

"I'm not lying. I don't lie, Mom; you know that."

"Then where did this box come from?"

"I can't tell you that."

"Why can't you?"

"I just can't."

"It doesn't belong to you. Who gave it to you?"

"Nobody gave it to me."

"Then how did you get it?"

"I . . . found it."

"Found it where?"

"I can't tell you. I promised."

"Promised who, if you found it?"

Silence.

"Did some boy give it to you? A boy at school?"

Silence.

"Emily, answer me. Did a boy give you this box? Do you have a boyfriend you haven't told us about?"

"No."

"So it wasn't a boy. One of your girlfriends?"

Headshake.

"Carla? Jeanne?"

Headshake.

"Kirstin?"

"Nobody. I found it."

Kerry glanced at me; the frustration in her face mirrored what must have been showing in mine.

My turn. I said, "Emily, you remember the talk we had about drugs?"

"I remember."

"You said you understood how dangerous they are, how much damage they can do. You swore you'd never use them."

"I do understand. I've never used drugs, not any kind, and I never will."

"Then explain the box."

"I already did, Dad. I found it."

"Where?"

"I can't tell you that. I promised."

"You keep saying that. Why would you make such a promise?"

Silence.

I couldn't think of anything else to say. Reason wasn't

working, and reason was the best way to deal with Emily on any subject. Threats, even if I believed in that kind of parental approach, wouldn't work, either. You couldn't force a girl like her into submission and confession. Punishment, constant badgering, would only cause her to withdraw.

It was already starting to happen; I could see it in the way she was sitting, eyes remote, face pale, shoulders hunched. Same hurt look, same unwillingness or inability to communicate, same form of self-defense, as when she'd first come to live with us—a fragile kid, badly damaged by the violent deaths of her parents and the lonely existence their sins had forced her to lead. Lost and hiding in a place deep inside herself that no one could reach. The fact that she'd been a near witness to an incident not long afterward, in which I'd been ambushed and nearly killed, had made her situation even worse: she'd had so much loss in her young life, she couldn't bear the thought of any more.

It had taken months of patience to bring her out of herself, to earn her complete trust. We had it now. Trust, loyalty, unconditional love. She was happy, much more outgoing and better socialized, with a bright future ahead of her. But she was still young and fragile; not enough time had passed for her wounds to fully heal. If we pushed her too hard, punished her too severely, we could drive her right back into that inner twilight world. We could lose her again.

And yet a thing like this, drugs, misplaced loyalty . . . we couldn't just ignore it or tiptoe around it. I glanced again at Kerry. Her expression said she was thinking along the same lines.

She said, "Emily, I know you understand why we're upset, why we're asking all these questions. Don't you have anything to say?"

"I'm sorry."

"For bringing drugs into this house."

"Yes. I swear I'll never do it again."

"Well, that's a start."

"Are you going to search my room again when I'm not home?"

"Not if you don't give us any cause to."

"I won't. Is it all right if I have the box?"

". . . What?"

"Not what's in it. Just the box."

"Why? Does it have some special meaning to you?"

"No. May I have it?"

"To do what with?"

"Give it back."

"To who?"

"The person it belongs to."

"So you know who lost the box."

"I . . . Yes."

"And you told this person you found it."

"Yes. But not that I opened it."

"Are you going to say that we did? That we know about the cocaine?"

"No, but I won't lie if I'm asked. May I have it?"

"No," I said, "you may not."

Emily started to say something, changed her mind. There was misery in her expression now, as if her emotions had begun to give her physical pain. Half a minute ticked away, during which time Shameless the cat wandered in and hopped up next to her. She clutched at him, pulled him close—something warm and furry to hang on to. Then, in a small voice, "May I be excused now?"

I melted a little. It wouldn't do any of us any good to keep her sitting there, keep hammering at her to no avail and watching her suffer. "All right, go ahead, but we're going to talk again later. I want you to think about telling the whole story when we do, think very hard."

"I won't break my promise, Dad. I can't do that."

Up and out of the room she went, carrying Shameless, her steps slow and not quite steady. I had the feeling that as soon as she was inside her room with the door shut she would start to cry. Soundlessly.

Kerry said, "Oh, Lord. You think she really did find that box?"

"She said she did and she doesn't lie."

"Then who is she protecting? Some boy?"

"I hope not."

"She's only thirteen. What if she's gotten herself involved with somebody older? What if she's already started having sex—"

"Hey. Don't go there."

"Don't tell me the thought hasn't crossed your mind."

". . . All right. But you be the one to ask her if it comes to that."

"I will."

"She won't admit to anything if it means breaking her promise."

"Oh, Lord. That damn teenage code: don't break promises; don't snitch." Kerry leaned across the table between our chairs, touched my hand. Her fingers were cold again. "What're we going to do?"

"I don't know. We can't force her to talk to us; we can't threaten her—you saw the way she looked."

"Calling up her friends' parents or talking to her teachers isn't the answer, either. All that'd do is open up a huge can of worms, with no guarantee of results."

"And turn her against us, drive her back inside herself."

"Well, we can't just pretend this didn't happen," Kerry said. "We have to get to the bottom of it. We have to do *something*."

Something. Sure. But what?

7

JAKE RUNYON

Since his relocation from Seattle to S.F. he'd spent a lot of time exploring and learning things about the city's neighborhoods, particularly the ones that presented potential dangers when you had to venture into them after dark. Dolores Park, the hub of the upper Mission District residential area, was one of these.

The park, two blocks long, one block wide, had steeply rolling lawns, acres of shade trees, winding paths, tennis courts, soccer field, kids' playground, dog-play area. People came from all over the city on weekends to take advantage of its attractions. In the late eighties and early nineties well-off Yuppies, lured by scenic views of the Mission and downtown and an easy commute, had bought up and renovated many of the old Victorians that rimmed the park.

Nice neighborhood . . . until the drug dealers moved in.

Pot sellers at first, targeting the students at nearby Mission High School, then another, rougher element dealing heroin, coke, meth. As many as forty dealers had been doing business in Dolores Park day and night in those days, Bill had told him.

And where you had hard drugs, you also had high stakes and violence; Runyon had seen it happen in Seattle when he'd been on the job there. One year there'd been eight shootings and two homicides in and around Dolores Park. Plus the fire-bombing of the home of a young couple who had tried to form an activist group to fight the dealers. Plus muggings, burglaries, intimidation of residents.

The SFPD and the city's park police had finally cracked down, cleaned the dealers out of the park and out of the Mission Playground down on 19th Street as well. Things had been quiet and stable again for a while. Then new problems started up. First it was homeless people camping in the park at night, panhandling aggressively by day. Then, recently, large groups began showing up on weekends and holidays, sanctioned and unsanctioned by the city: peace rallies, loud music festivals, freewheeling private parties that spawned public drunkenness, rowdy behavior, seminude sunbathing, loads of strewn trash, and damaged facilities and park property. The residents were up in arms again, for all the good it was doing. Most of them reportedly stayed out of the park on weekends and especially at night. Even with the hard-core dealers and homeless people gone, Latino gangbangers from the Mission and other lowlives still prowled it and muggings were not uncommon.

Few people were out on the lawns and paths when Runyon parked across the street on 19th. Too cold today, with the sea wind bringing in late-afternoon fog that hid the cityscape views behind tattered folds of gray. The Queen Anne Victorian that belonged to Arletta and Coy Madison was two doors down, its blue-on-blue paint job bright and fresh looking. Runyon went up the stoop, rang the bell. ID'd himself to the woman's voice that came through a speaker box.

There was a long pause before she said, "All right, I'll come down." She didn't sound too happy about it.

Pretty soon the door opened on a heavy chain and a narrow eye peered out at him through the aperture. He held his license up so the eye could read it. One blink was the only reaction.

She said, "What are you, a bounty hunter?"

"No. My agency operates on a straight fee basis."

"Same thing, if you're working for Troy's bondsman."

"It'd be easier if we could talk inside, Mrs. Madison."

"I can't tell you anything. Have you spoken to my husband?"

"Before I came here."

"If he doesn't know where Troy is, why do you suppose I do?"

"I don't suppose anything," Runyon said. "I just have a few questions."

She thought about it for ten seconds. Then she said, "Oh, all right, you may as well come in," and the chain rattled, the door opened all the way.

The rest of what went with the narrowed eye was older than Coy Madison, somewhere around thirty-five. She had an angular face dominated by a long, almost spadelike chin. Long brown hair was raggedly cut, as if she'd done it herself with a cracked mirror. She wore a not very clean smock over a man's Pendleton shirt and a pair of Levi's.

When Runyon was inside, she closed and locked and rechained the door and then turned past him and led him up a flight of stairs that ended in a short hallway. They went down that, through a couple of furnished rooms, and into a huge room at the rear that had been created by knocking out a wall or two and inserting three rows of skylights into the high canted roof. Artist's studio. A cluttered one full of sculptures

and paintings and the tools to create them, including an acety-
lene torch outfit.

He didn't know much about artworks, but he wasn't im-
pressed by what he saw here. The sculptures, more than twenty
of varying sizes, dominated the studio. To his untrained eye
they looked like nothing so much as weirdly misshapen root
and leaf vegetables made out of scraps of fused metal, glass,
straw, and some kind of ropy fibers—hemp, maybe. Big, little; long, short; fat, thin. Some of the tuberous ones had
filament-like ends that resembled roots or suckers. The paintings were all over on one side—three or four hung on the wall,
a partly finished one on an easel set up on a paint-stained drop
cloth, the rest leaning in uneven stacks. Unlike the sculptures,
they struck him as amateurish splatterings that had no form or
meaning, like the finger paintings kids made in grade school.

"Do you like them? My sculptures?" The words had an ex-
pectant, almost eager inflection. That was why she'd brought
him back here—to show off her work.

He said politely, "Interesting."

" 'Unique' is a better word, don't you think? Anselm Kiefer
was an early influence, but of course I've refined and developed my own vision and thematic concepts. His pieces tend
to be depressive, destructive, while mine are celebrations of
the fecundity of life."

She might have been speaking a foreign language. Runyon
nodded and said nothing.

"I've had eleven shows now and not a single knowledgeable
person has compared me to Kiefer. Some of the most eminent
critics in the art world have praised my creations as totally original. I'm starting to make a serious name for myself—finally,

after years of struggle. Just last month one of my best pieces, *Field of Desire,* sold for fifteen thousand dollars."

"That's a lot of money."

"Yes, but my work will be worth much more someday."

No false modesty in her. No humility of any kind.

"Are the paintings yours, too?"

She laughed, a half-delighted, half-derisive sound, as if he'd just told a juicy off-color story. "Good God, no. My husband's. Coy thinks he has artistic talent, but he doesn't—he'll never even rise to mediocrity. Self-delusion is just one of his faults."

Runyon was silent again.

"I suppose that sounds as if we don't get along very well," she said. "Sometimes we do. And sometimes he makes me so damn mad I could scream. When he calls me drunk from some bar downtown, for instance, bragging about a woman he's just picked up. He *knows* that drives me crazy."

Still nothing to say.

"Oh, not the crap about the women. They're lies, mostly. It's the drinking and the taunting that gets to me—he's so damn jealous of my success I swear his skin is developing a green tint." She sighed elaborately. "You're wondering why I stay married to him? Habit, I suppose. There's not much love left, but I do still care for him. God knows why. And of course he stays because now there's money, more money than either of us ever dreamed I'd be making."

Runyon had had enough of her personal life, her success, and her ego. He said, "Your brother-in-law, Mrs. Madison. The reason I'm here."

"Well, I have no idea where Troy is. I wish I did. You don't think I want him to get away, do you?"

"I hope not."

"You know I put up his bail money? Yes, of course you do. I let my husband talk me into it in a weak moment. They both promised me Troy would pay it back, but I didn't believe it."

"Then why agree? Thirty-five hundred is a lot of money."

"It used to be," Arletta Madison said. "Not anymore. I told you, my sculptures are starting to sell for large sums. *Very* large. And Troy is family. Neither he nor my husband may be worth much, but they're all the family I have."

And she got a bang out of lording it over them, Runyon thought. The kind of woman who used her success like a whip. He didn't like her much. But then he hadn't liked Coy Madison much, either.

He asked, "Can you give me the name of anyone who might help me find him? A friend of his or the woman he lives with?"

"That dreadful little tramp. She's the one who got him hooked on meth, you know."

"Is that right?"

"Six or seven years ago. He didn't use or sell hard drugs then, just a little recreational pot. He had a steady job with Bud before he met her."

"Bud?"

"Bud Linkhauser. Have you talked to him?"

"This is the first I've heard the name."

"Coy didn't say anything about Bud?"

"No."

"He and Troy and Bud grew up together in Bakersfield. I wonder why he didn't tell you that."

Runyon wondered why, too. He said, "Where can I find Bud Linkhauser?"

"He owns a trucking company in the East Bay. Hayward, I think. I don't have the address, but Coy probably does."

"I'll find it. What did your brother-in-law do for Linkhauser?"

"Mechanic." Condescending note in her voice, as if she considered mechanics several stations beneath her. "Troy has always been good with motors and things. Or he was before that Piper bitch got hold of him."

"What can you tell me about her?"

"Nothing. Except that she was probably the reason he jumped bail."

"Talked him into it, you mean?"

"Well, she wouldn't want her meal ticket to spend time in prison. Then what would she do for money and drugs? She's too ugly to sell her body. And probably diseased besides."

Runyon had now had enough of Arletta Madison, period. He gave her one of his cards and the standard call-if-you-think-of-anything-else line, and would have gotten out of there quick if she hadn't caught hold of his arm.

"Before you go," she said, "let me show you my latest piece. There, on the table by the door. It's good, isn't it—one of my best. I call it *Seedpod.*"

He looked at it for all of five seconds on his way out. It was a couple of feet long, round, with tapering ends, constructed of what seemed to be joined blobs of black-painted lead and studded with bits of straw and glass. He had a better name for it than hers. He'd have called it *Turd.*

Tamara provided the address and phone number for Linkhauser Trucking in Hayward, but the rest of what she had was sketchy. Jennifer Piper had been arrested five times, twice for prostitution, twice for possession of cocaine, and once for possession of crystal meth; she had no known relatives or associates other than Troy Madison, and Tamara hadn't been able to fill in her background yet beyond the past six years. Coy Madison had one DUI arrest, Arletta Madison no record of any kind. Background info on Bud Linkhauser would have to wait until tomorrow.

Runyon saved himself a long, wasted trip to Hayward by calling Linkhauser Trucking first. Bud Linkhauser was away on a run to the Central Valley, he was told, and not expected back until early tomorrow afternoon.

Bryn's weekend with her son hadn't gone well.

Runyon knew it as soon as she opened the door of her brown-shingled house on Moraga Street. It was in the way she looked at him, the unsmiling pensiveness of her expression. When he asked her about Bobby, her only response was to shake her head.

They went over to Taraval for dinner, as they did on most nights he saw her. She seldom left the house during daylight hours, but after being cooped up all day she preferred going out to eat to cooking at home. She didn't say a word on the way, lost inside herself. As always when she was like this, he made no effort to intrude on her silence in the car or in the coffee shop where they habitually ate. The place was crowded, but the diners were all neighborhood regulars who knew Bryn; that was why she'd become one of them. The two things she hated most were pity, especially from strangers, and being stared at while eating because of the difficulty she had in feeding herself.

Tonight she hardly touched her food. Wine was what she wanted; the first glass went down quick, in little sips so none of it would dribble out, and the second more slowly. That one seemed to relax her, finally loosened some of her reticence about the weekend.

"Bobby was so distant," she said. "He wouldn't let me hug him or even touch him, wouldn't make eye contact. Didn't want to go out anywhere. He spent most of the time alone in his room watching TV and playing video games."

"A kid phase. Or maybe he's having some problems in school."

"I hope that's all it is."

Runyon said, "You think his father might be trying to turn him against you?"

"I don't know. I can't believe Robert's that vindictive, but . . . I don't know him anymore. I guess I never did."

"It'll be better with Bobby next time."

"Will it? Oh, God, I can't stand the thought of losing him. If that happens . . ."

"The boy loves you. That's not going to change."

"It changed for you with your son."

"Different situation. Joshua and I never had a chance together from the beginning. His mother saw to that."

"Keep telling me I can't lose Bobby the same way," Bryn said. "If you say it often enough, maybe I'll start believing it."

Some nights when they were together, they went to a movie or took a drive somewhere. Not this one. Straight back to her house. But she didn't want to be alone; she asked him in. "Just for a while," she said. "I'd rather we didn't go to bed tonight; I'm not in the mood for sex."

"We don't always have to end up an evening in bed. I don't expect that."

"I know you don't. It's not that I don't want to be with you—I do. Just not tonight."

"No need to explain. I understand."

Inside, she poured herself another glass of wine. Drinking more than usual lately—not a good sign. But what could he say about it that wouldn't sound preachy? If alcohol helped her cope, all right, as long as she stayed with wine and kept it under control. He'd seen firsthand what booze could do to a woman who didn't have a self-governor. Andrea had let it control her, and it had destroyed their marriage, his relationship with Joshua, and finally herself.

They sat side by side in front of the gas-log fireplace, Bryn on his left as always so that the frozen side of her face was away from him. Close but not touching; she didn't like to be touched except by mutual consent. She was fond of classical music, but tonight it was silence and noncontact closeness she craved, neither of them saying anything, aware of each other but tuned in to their own thoughts. In a way, their intimacy was greater at times like this than when they were in bed together.

They spoke only once, when he shifted his weight from one hip to the other. She turned then and looked at him, a kind of wondering, searching look. "You're so good to me," she said.

"Why do you say that?"

"We always do what I want to. Or don't want to. Don't you ever get tired of giving in to my moods?"

"I don't see it as giving in."

"How do you see it?"

He shrugged. "I like to make you happy."

"Happy, Jake?"

"Comfortable, then. If you're comfortable, I'm comfortable."

Five-beat. Then, "You're not only good to me, you're good for me. You really are."

"I feel the same about you."

"You make me feel . . . safe. I need you right now, I don't know what I'd do without you, but . . ."

"But?"

"I'm not sure I deserve you."

"Come on, now. I'm nobody special."

"Oh yes, you are. What I should have said is that I'm not sure you deserve me . . . someone like me. A woman with a boatload of problems and insecurities. You should be with somebody normal—"

"That's enough of that," he said. "You are normal. And I don't want to be with anybody else."

"Right now you don't."

"Right now is enough. One day at a time, Bryn."

"Yes," she said. "One day at a time."

8

TAMARA

Doctor Easy's name was Hawkins, Eugene Z. Hawkins, D.C.M. And he was a scumbag.

She ran him through six different databases and several linked sources, including the *Chronicle* and a couple of other Bay Area newspapers, and Felice ran him through the SFPD and NJIS files. Routine info at first. Age forty-two. Twice married, once divorced, no children. Doctor of Chiropractic Medicine for nearly twenty years, first in San Jose, then in Cupertino, then in S.F. for the last eleven. Shared offices with another chiropractor on Ocean Avenue. Lived with his second wife in a home in Monterey Heights, drove a Lexus, seemed to be well off financially.

The rest of his background record told a different story.

Arrested in San Jose in 1994 on a charge of soliciting a male vice cop for sex in a public restroom—an undercover sting like the one that'd caught the Idaho senator a while back. Protested his innocence, same as the senator, went to court, and walked on a technicality.

Accused by a woman patient in 1997 of inappropriate

touching during soft-tissue therapy, whatever that was. Not arrested because she changed her mind, or had it changed for her, and dropped the charges. Nearly cost him his license to practice and was probably the reason for his move from Cupertino to S.F.

Arrested in Petaluma in 2000, in another sting operation—this one for Internet solicitation of sex with what he believed to be a sixteen-year-old male. Nabbed when he showed up for a prearranged date at a motel. Protested his innocence again, said it was all a misunderstanding, but this time he didn't have any wiggle room. Convicted, fined, forced to register as a sex offender. That was when his first wife divorced him.

Accused by the California Franchise Tax Board in 2004 of failure to pay adequate state income tax over the previous five years. Found guilty and heavily fined.

Yeah, a scumbag.

Question was, what else was he? Just a bisexual member of the sports club? A scam victim of the phony Lucas? Or a scammer himself?

D ecision time.

Doctor Easy was a solid lead, the only one she had, but she couldn't risk bracing him herself. No way of knowing if the phony Lucas had told him about her, maybe even described her. Hawkins wouldn't be likely to tell a woman anything anyway, especially not about the down-low club.

Like it or not, what she needed was a man—a good-looking male op who could pass for a successful, bisexual businessman.

And he had to be black.

That meant bringing in an outsider, a borrow from one of

the other agencies in S.F. or the Bay Area. Trouble was, full-time field ops were usually kept as busy as she kept Jake Runyon; finding one who looked the part and had a hole in his caseload might not be easy. A part-timer was the best bet.

Well, she knew one possible—and he fit the profile. Deron Stewart. Part-timer for several different agencies, mainly Matt Bannerman's. Good record—seven years with the California Highway Patrol, eight years with a big national outfit in their S.F. office before the economic crunch squeezed him out—but no luck so far in landing a staff job anywhere since. But did she want to work with him? The man was a pussy hound; one meeting with him and she'd known that from the way he talked, swaggered a little in her presence, and roamed his eyes over her body. Egotistical cocksman types turned her off. Sniff, sniff, sniff around every woman they met from eight to eighty, black, white, or yellow, crippled, blind, or crazy.

All right, then. Make some calls, see if she could borrow somebody else.

The calls produced zip. Either nobody employed the kind of man she was after or if they did, he wasn't available on short notice. So it would have to be Deron Stewart . . . if she could get him. She called Matt Bannerman, and he said Stewart wasn't doing any work for him right now, or for any other agency that he knew about. He gave her two phone numbers, cell and home. She picked the cell first.

"Deron Stewart here."

She ID'd herself and the agency. "You interviewed with us for a field op position a couple of years ago."

"And didn't get it. I remember."

"Not because you weren't qualified."

"You hired a white man instead."

"Race had nothing to do with our decision."

"Uh-huh. I've heard that before. What can I do for you, Ms. Corbin?"

"A job, if you're interested. Short-term, one or two days probably, but it pays top wages."

"What kind of job?"

"Fraud case. Involving African Americans."

"Which is why you need me."

"Yes or no, Mr. Stewart?"

"What is it you want me to do? And how soon?"

"Right away," Tamara said. "If you want the job, come on over and I'll give you the details."

"South Park offices now, right? Nice location. You must be doing pretty well."

"Two ninety South Park. How soon can you be here?"

"Forty-five minutes," he said. "Less, if the traffic cooperates."

Deron Stewart may not have been working steadily, but he dressed as if he were. Charcoal pin-striped suit, pale blue shirt with gold cuff links, a yellow patterned tie. Big gold and onyx ring and a gold-banded wristwatch that looked expensive. Attractive enough, if you liked your men slick. Piercing eyes almost as black as his skin, with that hungry glint in them. One of those fat-toothed smiles that probably had some women reaching to unhook their bras when he turned it on them. Pure hound. Like Vonda had said once about a guy she knew, he'd screw a board fence if the knothole was in the right place.

He looked her over pretty good when he came in, not being obvious about it—cool and practiced, sizing up the goods and his chances of adding her to his scorecard. Tamara pretended not to notice. If he hit on her, and sooner or later he probably would, straight out or sly, she could handle him. Wasn't any man after the phony Lucas who'd mess her up again. The way she felt right now, she didn't care if she spent the rest of her life celibate as a nun.

She sat Stewart down in the client's chair in her office, with her desk between them. Nobody else there but the two of them; Bill and Jake and Alex were all out and not likely to come back until late, if at all. Otherwise she'd've arranged to meet Stewart somewhere else.

He sat relaxed and attentive, one leg crossed over the other and those glinty eyes fixed on her face, as she sketched out the case details and what she wanted him to do. Told him pretty much everything except the personal angle. Working the case for a client, she said. He may have been a hound, but he was no-nonsense when it came to business. Let her do the talking, except to put in a question now and then when something wasn't clear to him. Quick study, too. Took it all in, processed it, read it back to her after she was done.

She said, "Think you can play the part?"

"Sure. No problem."

"Low-key. Don't come on too strong."

"Don't worry; I can handle it. Long as you're sure Hawkins and Zeller are on the down low and this sports fan club is for switch-hitters only."

"Sure enough. One look at you in person, you'll get an invitation. Guaranteed."

Stewart's smile bent downward a little. "Backhanded compliment. Do I look like a switch-hitter to you?"

"None of my business what you do in private."

"One hundred percent hetero," he said. "For the record."

His horny eyes moved over her face like a caress. She ignored them. "Go ahead and make the call. I'll listen in in my partner's office. Get a take on Hawkins's reaction."

"Suppose he won't talk to me."

"Then you'll have to get in to see him at his office. Or hang around and brace him when he leaves."

Stewart made the call on her phone. Asked the woman who answered if he could speak to Dr. Hawkins on a personal matter. "My name's Stewart, Deron Stewart. Tell him we met at the sports show at Moscone Center last month."

Three minutes passed. Come on, Easy, Tamara thought, pick up, talk to the man. And there was a click and a reedy voice said, "This is Dr. Hawkins."

"Deron Stewart, Doctor. You probably don't remember me—"

"No, I'm sorry, I don't. We met at the Moscone sports show, you said?"

"That's right. I talked to a lot of people that day and I guess you did, too."

"Yes. Very crowded event."

"You said to call you Doctor Easy."

"Did I? Well."

"You were with a friend, a man named . . . Heller, was it?"

"Zeller. Yes." Pause. "What can I do for you, Mr. Stewart?"

"Well, I've been thinking about that club you mentioned." Stewart cleared his throat. He was playing it just right. Softened his voice, put in a little nervousness but not too much. "The one you and Zeller belong to."

Ten seconds of silence. Hawkins trying to remember. Then, "Yes?"

"Five members and there was room for another man. I said I didn't think I'd be interested, but . . . I've changed my mind. If there's still room."

"There is. For the right man."

"Compatible, you mean. The club . . . all brothers?"

"That's right. Businessmen, professional people like myself. What business are you in, Mr. Stewart?"

"Computers. Bayside Computer Sales and Service. One of our sidelines is providing computers to schools, mainly those in impoverished sections of the Bay Area."

"I see. Admirable."

"Married, two kids. But my wife and I . . . well, I won't go into that." Stewart cleared his throat again. "Anyhow, I think I might fit in. I've been a sports nut all my life, all kinds, especially football and basketball, I like talking sports to other knowledgeable guys, and I . . . well, I'm married, as I said, but I like to get out once in a while, have a good time with guys who feel the same. You know what I mean?"

"Perhaps."

"So do you think I might fit in?"

"Perhaps," Hawkins said again.

"Well . . . maybe we could get together, get to know each other, talk it over. Zeller, too, if he wants to join us."

Four-beat. Then, "I think that might be arranged. Suppose you let me have your phone number, Mr. Stewart."

"Deron. Call me Deron."

"Let me have your number and I'll get back to you."

"How soon?"

"Soon."

"Before the club meets again?"

"Yes. Before then."

Hawkins provided his cell number and they ended the conversation. Tamara reslotted Bill's phone, went back through the connecting door. Stewart grinned up at her from the client's chair.

"How was I?" he asked.

Probably the same question he asked his conquests as soon as they finished doing the nasty. Self-centered types like him always cared more about their performance than anything or anybody else. And if he got any rating less than a rave, he'd blame the woman for being a lousy lay.

Tamara said, "Believable." Why give him any more satisfaction?

"Yeah, I thought he bought it. I'll be hearing from him."

"That company name you gave, Bayside Computer Sales and Service—"

"My brother-in-law's company. I've used it before. He'll know what to say if Hawkins checks up."

Stewart's attitude toward women was sexist lousy and his ego overinflated, but she had to admit he was good at his job. Some agency should've put him on full-time by now. Racism? She'd never come up against any of that crap in her dealings with other agencies, but that didn't mean it wasn't there under the surface.

He said, "I think Hawkins will agree to the get-together. You?"

"No reason why he shouldn't." Unless the phony Lucas or somebody else talked him out of it. "But I'm not so sure about Zeller."

"I figure he'll want to scope me out, too. Only problem I

can see is that I'll be a stranger to them. Might lead to questions, suspicions."

"It's been over a month since the sports show," Tamara said, "and Moscone was packed that day. Not too likely they'll remember everybody they talked to."

"Not even a handsome guy like me?"

She let that pass. "You ought to be able to convince them."

"Never been in a situation yet I couldn't handle."

"Okay. When you hear from Hawkins and you've got a time and place, let me know right away. My cell, day or night."

"Will do," Stewart said. "If Zeller does show up, you want me to follow him afterward, find out where he lives? Tail jobs are my specialty. He'll never know I'm there."

"Uh-uh. You leave Zeller to me. And take along a voice-activated recorder so there's a record of everything that's said."

"Your client must really want this guy put away."

"Oh yeah," Tamara said. "Real bad."

9

I didn't feel like going to work on Wednesday morning. Neither Kerry nor I had gotten much sleep, and I was tired, depressed, cranky. My curmudgeon's mode, she calls it. But she wasn't in much better shape. This thing with Emily had both of us down and reeling.

The kid had stayed in her room all last evening, lying on her bed with Shameless beside her and her iPod headphones plugged into her ears. Music was her passion—she wanted to be a singer and she had the voice to make it happen; when she was upset, she retreated into music as completely as she withdrew into herself. Even if we'd taken the iPod away from her, we wouldn't have been able to reach her. She wouldn't eat, wouldn't communicate. Kerry went in once and asked her point-blank if she was experimenting with sex. Emily said no, of course not, and looked hurt again, and that was the end of that.

Breakfast this morning hadn't been any more productive. She'd sat at the table with her eyes on her plate, picking at her food, speaking in polite monosyllables when she spoke at all. Kerry had brought up the cocaine again, quietly, but Emily's nonanswers were the same as the night before. "I promised

I wouldn't tell. I can't break my promise. I've never tried drugs of any kind."

I believed the last statement. She simply did not lie; it wasn't in her nature. If there were such a thing as an Honest Teenager of the Year Award, she'd win it hands down. Reassuring, but there was still the box and that tube of coke. And her steadfast and misplaced loyalty to whoever they belonged to.

What do you do in a situation like this? How do you find the answers without stirring up a hornet's nest?

What the hell do you do?

Despite my lack of enthusiasm, I went to work anyway. That had always been my escape—Kerry's, too—from unpleasant and difficult personal problems. Retreat into the job the way Emily retreated into music and other people buried themselves in books or films or booze.

Patterson Realty Company, Inc., was a storefront hole-in-the-wall on Balboa near 46th Avenue, within hailing distance of the Great Highway and Ocean Beach. Coming to this part of the city always gave me pangs of nostalgia, even on a day and in a mood like this one. It was where Playland-at-the-Beach used to be, and Playland—a ten-acre amusement park in the grand old style, once the largest on the West Coast—had been where I'd spent a good portion of my youth.

Playland. Some exciting place when you were young and full of piss and vinegar. Attractions galore. Laughing Sal, the gap-toothed, red-haired plaster icon at the entrance, whose cackling mechanical laugh scared the hell out of generations of little kids. Shooting galleries. Sideshow lures that included a two-headed duckling and a radiation-deformed carp. The

Fun House with its moveable sidewalk and "spinning wheel" and mirror maze. The creaky old Big Dipper roller coaster, the Whip, the Aeroplane Swing, the Dodg-'Em cars, and other rides. The penny arcade called Knotty Peek and the Tip-a-Troll and Ring-the-Bottle games.

The first date I went on as a teenager was to Playland. And the night I lost my virginity, in the backseat of my old Chevy coupe parked out on Land's End, was after another Playland date—both the girl and me with our hormones raging after a succession of thrill rides on the Big Dipper and the Whip. Memory's a funny thing. I remember the girl's name, Cricket, and the sensations she stirred in me, but her face is dim and everything else about her is a total blank; yet all I have to do is close my eyes and I can see Playland exactly as it was, in every detail—I can even smell the popcorn and saltwater taffy, the hot dogs and bull-pup tamales, all the rich odors mixed together with the tang of cold salt air, and I can hear the shrieks and excited laughter of the kids.

All gone now. Nothing left of the park except bright ghost-images in the memories of graybeards like me. The city closed Playland down in the late sixties, allowed it to sit abandoned for a few years, and then demolished it on Labor Day weekend of 1972. Condos and rental apartment buildings took over those ten acres and more besides: Beachfront Luxury Living, Spectacular Views. Yeah, sure. Luxuriously cold gray weather and spectacular weekend views of Ocean Beach and its parking areas jammed with rowdy teenagers and beer-guzzling adult children.

It made me sad, looking at those characterless buildings, thinking about Playland. Getting old. Sure sign of it when you started lamenting the long-dead past, glorifying it as if it were some kind of Utopia when you knew damned well it hadn't been. Maybe so, maybe so. But nobody could convince me Beachfront Luxury Living condos were better than Laughing Sal, the Big Dipper, and Knotty Peek, or that some of the dead past wasn't a hell of a lot more desirable than most of the screwed-up present.

There were two desks inside the Patterson Realty Company offices, each of them occupied when I walked in. The man was long and lean, forty or so, wearing a brown suit that didn't fit him very well, owner of a gap-toothed smile and greedy eyes that locked onto yours and hung on as if they couldn't bear to let go. The woman was a few years younger, with short hair dyed henna red, a thin red mouth, and too much makeup on her narrow face; her choice of clothing wasn't too appealing, either, a pale green pantsuit and yellow blouse that clashed with her hair. Allan and Doris Patterson. First impression: real estate bottom-feeders. Just the kind you'd expect to find in the front row at a city-held tax auction.

They were glad-hand friendly until I told them who I was and that I was investigating the harassment of Margaret Abbott. No more smiles, then. Allan Patterson's gaze quit hanging on to mine and never quite came back again. Off with the sheep's clothing and out jumped the wolves with fangs bared.

"That Alvarez woman hired you, I suppose," Patterson said with more than a little nastiness.

"My client's name is privileged information."

"Oh, sure. Privileged. Damn her, she's out to get us."

"Why would Helen Alvarez be out to get you?"

He said, "She's an old busybody who ought to mind her own business," as if that answered the question.

"The point is, Mrs. Abbott is being harassed and I'm trying to get to the bottom of it."

"Well, my God," Doris Patterson said, "why come to us about that? We don't have anything to do with it."

"We're not vandals," he added. "Do we look like vandals?"

Loaded question. I didn't answer it.

His wife said, "What earthly good would it do us to subject the Abbott woman to petty vandalism? We've already lost her property, thanks to that bleeding-heart judge."

"I'm not here to accuse you of anything," I said. "I just want to ask you a few questions."

"We don't have anything to say to you. We don't know anything; we don't want to know anything."

"And furthermore, you don't give a damn."

"You said that, I didn't. Anyway, why should we?"

"Because an old woman in trouble deserves a little compassion?"

"Not that crazy old woman. Or her even crazier friend. Not after all we've been put through, all the legal fees they cost us."

Patterson said, "If you or the Alvarez woman try to imply that we're involved, or that we're in any way exploiters of the chronologically gifted, we'll sue for defamation of character. I mean that—we'll sue."

"Exploiters of the what?" I said.

"You heard me. The chronologically gifted."

Christ, I thought. Old people hadn't been old people—or elderly people—for some time, but I hadn't realized they were no longer even senior citizens. Now they were the "chronologically gifted"—the most asinine example of newspeak I had yet encountered. The ungifted agency types who coined such euphemisms ought to be excessed, transitioned, outsourced, offered voluntary severance, or provided with immedate career-change opportunities. Or better yet, subjected to permanent chronological interruption.

So much for the Pattersons. A waste of time coming here; you couldn't get them to admit to anything even remotely illegal or unethical, no matter what you said or did. All the interview had accomplished was to confirm Helen Alvarez's low opinion of the pair. I'd be satisfied if it turned out they had something to do with the vandalism and scare tactics, but hell, where was their motive? Opportunistic assholes, yes; childishly vindictive tormenters, no. And unfortunately there is no law against being an asshole in today's society. If there was, 10 percent of the population would be in jail and another 10 percent would be on the cusp.

Charley Doyle, Mrs. Abbott's nephew, worked for a glass-service outfit in Daly City. I called to see if he was in, and he wasn't: out on a job and not expected to return until late afternoon.

I spent the rest of the morning checking in with Helen Alvarez—no further incidents at the Abbott home—and then interviewing several of Mrs. Abbott's neighbors. None of them had anything enlightening to tell me. A few had opinions, though, as to who was responsible for the vandalism; the Pattersons topped the list, followed by Everett Belasco's "bums or street punks."

I had no appetite, so I skipped lunch and drove downtown to the agency. Tamara had promised to do some background checking on the principals in the case and I thought there might be something in the data to give me a direction to move in. But she wasn't there; Jake Runyon was holding down the fort. The background info wasn't there, either. Usually she prints out Internet material, my computer skills being what they aren't, and leaves the papers on my desk. No papers today. And no note of explanation.

I asked Runyon, "Tamara say when she'd be back from lunch?"

"No. Just to lock up if she wasn't here by the time I was ready to leave. Everything okay with her?"

"Why do you ask?"

"She doesn't seem herself lately. Took a bite out of me this morning for a mistake in my Bower case report that wasn't a mistake."

"I've noticed it, too," I said. "Distracted. Worked up about something personal she doesn't want to talk about, probably. She didn't do background checks I asked for yesterday—and that's a first for her."

Runyon had nothing to say to that. He was reticent when it came to personal matters himself. The best field investigator I'd ever worked with, but a private man, inwardly focused much of the time, weighed down with grief over the lingering cancer death of his second wife a couple of years ago. But lately it seemed as if he was finally starting to let go of his grief. He was more relaxed, less determined to wrap himself cocoonlike in his work. Reason for the change: Bryn Darby, the graphic designer and artist he'd met a couple of months ago. Their relationship seemed to be developing legs; for his sake, I hoped so.

Runyon went off to interview somebody on the bail-jump case he was working for Abe Melikian, and I went back into my office to take care of some routine business. But I wasn't alone for long. Ten minutes later, Tamara banged in.

"Banged" is the right word. She shouldered open the door, slammed it shut behind her, and stomped into her office. I got up to look in through the open connecting door. She was shedding her coat; instead of hanging it up, she pitched it onto the client's chair; and when it slid off onto the floor, she left it there. Good Tamara was on vacation again, Bad Tamara once more the temp in residence.

"Hey," I said, "what's up, kiddo?"

"Nothing," she said. She sounded frustrated as well as grumpy. "Waiting's a bitch."

"Waiting for what?"

"Just waiting, that's all."

"If you want to talk—"

"I don't. Just want to get back to work."

"On those background checks I asked for yesterday?"

"What? Oh . . . yeah. Meant to do them this morning, but I got sidetracked."

"I'd appreciate it if you'd do them now. Unless you've got more pressing business."

"No. Get right on it."

I felt that I ought to say something more to her, try to draw her out a little, but you can't get through to Bad Tamara. Reason, subtle probing, the fatherly or mentor approach . . . none of it works. All you can do is ride out the storm until Good Tamara decides to come home again.

10

It didn't take Tamara long to run the checks on the various individuals I'd encountered so far in the Abbott case. All but two had spotless records, the Pattersons among them unless you counted questionable ethics and business practices. The other two had only minor blemishes on their records, though one of the blemishes was of some potentially relevant interest.

Charley Doyle, the nephew, had been arrested twice, once on a D & D charge and once, five years ago, for causing a traffic accident while drunk that landed a forty-four-year-old Millbrae woman in the hospital with minor injuries. For the latter he'd paid a hefty fine and lost his driver's license for a year; he was lucky the injured woman hadn't sued him. Mrs. Alvarez's brother, Leonard Crenshaw, was a parking scofflaw—twenty-two unpaid parking tickets dating back several years—and had been arrested once at age eighteen on a charge of malicious mischief. He and two other dummies had broken into an abandoned house in the Excelsior District and trashed it for no reason other than pure deviltry. A judge had ordered him and his cohorts to pay damages and sentenced them to two hundred hours each of community service.

Once a vandal, always a vandal? Pretty thin, but something

to keep in mind just the same. And to ask Helen Alvarez and Crenshaw about the next time I saw them.

At a little after three I drove out to Dependable Glass Service, on Mission a half mile or so beyond the San Francisco–Daly City line, to see what I could find out from Charley Doyle. I'd been told he'd be back in the shop by three thirty, and he had been. But then he'd immediately signed out for the day; I missed him by five minutes. Glaziers evidently had the same sweetheart thirty-six-hour workweek as plumbers and other union tradespeople.

I told one of the office workers that I needed to talk to Doyle on an urgent matter regarding his aunt. That bought me his home address, which was also in Daly City. In my car I looked up the street and a route on one of the sheaf of maps I keep in the glove box. Newer cars nowadays are equipped with GPS navigators that make printed maps pretty much obsolete; Kerry has one in hers. But mine is fifteen years old, and even when I trade it in, as I figure I'll need to do fairly soon, it'll likely be for a used pre-GPS model. I'm a Luddite when it comes to modern technological advancements. A lighted computer screen on my dashboard and a disembodied mechanical voice giving me directions and chastising me if I didn't follow them to the letter would only make me uncomfortable. I prefer to get my directions the old-fashioned way.

Doyle lived in a two-story, twelve-unit apartment building at least thirty years old, its stucco and wood façade showing signs of advanced age and not much TLC. What had once been a front lawn bisected by a cracked concrete path was now two rectangles of brown hay almost tall enough for harvesting. I went into an open foyer and found the mailbox marked:

C. Doyle and pushed the the bell button. Nobody answered the ring.

I was about to give it up when a man came clumping down the inner stairs and out through the entrance door. Little guy about my age, who looked as if he'd had the same hard and neglected life as his place of residence: shaggy white hair, untrimmed white beard, yellowish eyes with tiny threads of blood swimming in the whites. He gave me an uninterested glance, would have brushed right on by if I hadn't moved a little to block his way.

"Excuse me," I said. "I'm looking for one of your neighbors, Charley Doyle."

"So?"

"He doesn't seem to be home."

"So?"

Like talking to the former vice president. Same snappish, snotty tone. "Would you have any idea where he might be? Some place he goes after work?"

"Why?"

"I need to talk to him. It's about his aunt."

"So?"

"Look, I'm just trying—"

"Fat Leland's," he said.

". . . How's that again?"

"Bar."

"Where?"

"Mission."

"Where on Mission?"

He threw me a *go fuck yourself* look, stepped around me, and went away.

I said, "So long, Dick," but if he heard me he didn't care enough to respond.

F at Leland's was less than a mile from Dependable Glass Service. Typical neighborhood blue-collar tavern, moderately crowded and noisy when I walked in. I wedged in at the bar, caught the barman's attention, ordered a draft Anchor Steam, and when he brought it asked if Charley Doyle was there.

He was. Sitting in a booth with a hefty, big-chested blonde who reminded me of a woman my former partner, Eberhardt, once mistakenly came close to marrying. Schooners of beer, two mostly full, two empty, sat wetly on the table between them. But all they had eyes for at the moment was each other. They were snuggled in close together, rubbing on each other and swapping beer-flavored saliva. They didn't like it when I slid in across from them, and Doyle liked it even less when I told him who I was and why I was there.

"I don't know nothing about it," he said. He was a big guy with a beer belly, loose, wet lips, and dim little eyes. *Two brain cells and one of them is usually passed out drunk,* Helen Alvarez had said. Good description. "What you want to bother me for?"

"I thought you might have some idea of who's behind the vandalism."

"Not me. Old lady Alvarez thinks it's them real estate people that tried to steal my aunt's house. Why don't you go talk to them?"

"I already did. They deny any involvement."

"Lying bastards," he said.

"Maybe. You been out to see your aunt lately?"

"Not since I fixed her busted window. Why?"

"Well, you're her only relative. She could use some moral support."

"Some what?"

"Comfort. A friendly face."

"Yeah, well, she's got Alvarez and her brother to take care of her. She don't need me hanging around." He helped himself to a long pull from his schooner, smacked his lips. The blonde nuzzled his shoulder and gave him a vacuously adoring look. "Besides, she gives me the creeps."

"Your aunt does? Why?"

"She's about half-nuts. What's that disease old people get? *Al* something?"

"Alzheimer's. But she's not afflicted with that."

"Afflicted," Doyle said, as if it were a dirty word he didn't quite understand.

"She's not senile, either. Pretty much in possession of all her faculties, I'd say."

"All her what?"

I sighed. "Brains."

"That's what you think. How many times you talked to her?"

"Once."

"Once. Hah. Spend time over there, you'll see what I mean. Babbles on about crazy stuff. Ghosts, for Chrissake. Her dead husband's friggin' ghost."

"Tell me, Mr. Doyle, do you stand to inherit her estate?"

"Huh?"

"Do you get her house and property when she dies?"

His dim little eyes showed faint glimmers of light. "Yeah, that's right. So what? You think it's me doing all that crap to her?"

"I'm just asking questions."

"Yeah, well, I don't like your questions. You can't pin it on me."

"I'm not trying to pin anything on you. Trying to get at the truth, that's all."

"Told you, man, I got no truth for you. I got nothing for you." He sucked at the schooner again, dribbling a little beer down his chin this time. "Last Saturday night, when them rosebushes of hers was dug up, I was in Reno with a couple of buddies. And when that damn cat got poisoned, me and Melanie here was together the whole night at her place." He nudged the blonde with a dirty elbow. "Wasn't we, kid?"

Melanie giggled, belched delicately, said, "Whoops, excuse me," and giggled again. Then she frowned and said, "What'd you ask me, honey?"

"Wednesday night," Doyle said.

"What about Wednesday night?"

"We was together the whole night, wasn't we? At your place?"

"Oh, sure," Melanie said, "all night," and the giggle popped out again. "You're a real man, Charley, that's what you are."

Doyle nodded once, emphatically, and said to me, "There, you see? You satisfied now?"

"For the time being. But I might need corroborating evidence later on."

"Huh?"

I slid out of the booth and left the two of them sucking beer and rubbing on each other again. Once of those perfect matches, Doyle and Melanie, that you know exist but fortunately seldom encounter. Four tiny brain cells, drunk or sober, united against the world.

. . .

Kerry wasn't home yet—she had a late meeting at Bates and Carpenter, one of many that had become necessary since her promotion to agency vice president—but Emily was there, working on her computer. We'd instructed her to come straight home after school and I didn't have to ask her if she'd obeyed. When she was told to do something, she did it without failure or question. Always had until this drug business, anyway.

She had a thin little smile for me, but the sadness and hurt still showed in her eyes. I asked her what she was working on; she said research for an American history project. Two minutes on that subject and then we got down to what was on both our minds.

On the way home I'd worked up a different approach than the ones we'd used before—an appeal to her good judgment and common sense. "Emily, I know you hate to break promises, but this cocaine business is different—it's a serious adult issue. A promise to your parents is more important than one to a friend or schoolmate."

Her gaze held steady on mine. "I didn't break my promise to you."

"Not about using drugs, but bringing cocaine home amounts to the same thing. Unless you had an innocent reason for doing it. Did you?"

"Yes."

"Then tell me what it was."

"I can't. I don't want anyone to be hurt."

"It's too late for that. You're hurt; Kerry and I are hurt."

"Not as bad as they'll be hurt."

"They? More than one person?"

"No. Just . . . no."

They. Meaning "he or she." Grammar was one of Emily's best subjects; she'd used the plural on purpose, to disguise the person's sex.

What I said next went against my principles, but if it was the only way to pry the truth out of her, then I was willing to make the sacrifice. Kerry would be, too. You can't police the entire world, especially the complex and volatile segment inhabited by teenagers. "It doesn't have to be that way, Emily. I'll make *you* a promise. If all you did was bring that box home to protect a friend, and that friend isn't pressuring you in any way, then all you have to do is tell us who and why and we'll let the matter drop. No one will ever know you told us."

She shook her head. "That's a promise you wouldn't keep, Dad."

"Why do you say that? I'm not a promise breaker any more than you are."

"I know, but . . ."

"But what?"

Silence. Her gaze shifted to the computer screen. You could almost see her withdrawing again, the muscles in her face tightening, the remoteness coming back into her eyes.

"Tell me about the box," I said.

"What about it?"

"Did you talk to the person it belongs to today?"

No immediate response. Thinking about it, and squirming a little in her chair as if the memory was causing her some discomfort. It was almost a minute before she said, "The person I thought it belonged to, yes."

"Thought it belonged to?"

"It doesn't. It's not theirs, the box or what was in it. I was wrong."

"You sure about that?"

"I believe them," she said, but there was something in her voice that made me think she might not be completely convinced.

"Did the person ask you what happened to the cocaine?"

"Yes."

"What did you say?"

"I told them. How Mom found the box . . . everything."

"Were they upset?"

"Sort of."

"Did they want you to get it back? Turn it over to them?"

"No, they're not like that. They don't have any idea who it belongs to."

"Ask you not to tell us their name?"

". . . Yes. But it's not what you think. They don't want anyone to get the wrong impression."

"That they're the one doing coke, you mean."

"Yes. Because they're not."

"Emily, where did you find the box?

"I can't tell you that."

"Emily . . ."

"You'll know if I tell you and I can't . . . I *can't*."

"All right. You didn't see it being lost, did you?"

"No. I found it afterward, later."

"Then why did you think it belonged to this person you talked to today?"

Headshake.

"Did somebody else tell you who owned it?"

"No. I . . . saw it once before."

"In this person's possession?"

"Yes."

"Why didn't you go to the person right away after you found it?"

"I couldn't."

"Why couldn't you?"

Headshake. Like trying to pry out splinters with a fork.

I said, "Did you open the box before you brought it home?"

"No. Not until after I got home. I wish I hadn't; I wish I'd never seen what was inside."

"Would you have returned the box with the cocaine still in it?"

"I don't think so. I might've just thrown it away. Or come to you and Mom, asked you what to do."

"But once you were sure whose box it was, you felt you couldn't do that."

"No, I . . . No."

"Why? Why is this person so special to you?"

"Please, Dad. Please. They didn't do anything wrong, I didn't do anything wrong, I don't want them to be hurt." The raspy breath she drew seemed to make her small body tremble. "I just want everything to be the way it was before."

"That can't happen, Emily."

"I know it can't," she said, and she started to cry. Suddenly, without sound—tears leaking out of her eyes, glistening silver on her smooth cheeks. My immediate impulse was to go around the desk and take her in my arms, hold her, tell her everything would be all right. But it was the wrong thing to do; the time for comfort and reassurance was after confession, not before.

I left her alone, went and sat in my chair in the living room, and tried to make some sense of the few little snippets of information I'd gotten out of her. She'd found the box somewhere, had seen it before and knew who it belonged to, but hadn't known what was in it until she got it home. All right. But why had she later gone to him or her and promised to keep the person's identity secret? Why so protective?

An idea occurred to me, one I should have thought of before. I'd locked the box in the mini-safe in Kerry's and my bedroom closet; the little plastic vial was still in it, but the cocaine was long gone down the sewer. There was a strong halogen lamp on the desk in Kerry's home office, a twin to the one in Emily's room; I took the box in there, shut the door, switched the lamp on, and emptied out the cotton and the plastic vial. Then I rummaged around in the desk drawer until I found her big fold-out magnifying glass.

On the first squint through the glass I couldn't make out anything on the inside or outside of the box except scratches, wear marks, and a couple of tiny dents. I looked again, examining both sides of the lid, all four outer sides, the bottom. Nothing. One more time—

Something.

I was holding the box at an upward angle, with one lower corner in the center of the lens. What had seemed like random scratches before, one on each lower corner edge, took on a different aspect then. And I was seeing what Emily must have seen when she studied the box as I was doing now. Smart kid—smarter in some ways than her sometimes slow adoptive father.

Initials. Two of them, etched into the soft bronze-colored tin, probably a long time ago, because handling and rubbing had made them virtually invisible to the naked eye.

Z.U.

My first impulse was to go back into Emily's room and confront her again. Wrong move; I didn't do it. She wouldn't tell me who Z.U. was.

There was another way to find out. *Z.U.* was a fairly uncommon set of initials, and whoever owned them figured to be somebody Emily knew at Whitney Middle School. As Tamara said often enough, you can find out anything on the Internet if you have a starting point—anything at all.

11

TAMARA

Deron Stewart called her cell late Thursday morning. Pretty fast response time, but she'd hoped it would be even faster—last night, before she went to bed. She hadn't slept much. Pins and needles, waiting. Shouldn't be this wired; the phony Lucas hadn't hurt her that badly, not nearly as much as he could have. But she couldn't help how she felt. Hunger for revenge can do funny things to you.

Bill was in his office, with the connecting door open as usual. She told Stewart to hold on, took her phone out through the anteroom into the hallway. Nobody out there. She moved away from the door, over toward the stairs.

"Okay, go ahead."

"Hawkins just called," Stewart said. "Suggested we meet for drinks tonight at six o'clock."

"With Zeller?"

"I asked him that; he said he wasn't sure. So I left it there. Didn't want to push him."

The right way to handle it. But frustration dug at her again anyway. "Where're you meeting Doctor Easy?"

"Place called the Twilight Lounge, on Ocean near his office."

"Twilight Lounge. Okay. Make sure you take the voice-activated recorder along."

"No worries. I've got it covered."

"Call me afterward, soon as you're alone."

"Right. You sure you don't want me to follow Zeller if he shows up?"

"I'm sure," she said.

The Twilight Lounge was in the three-block business section of Ocean Avenue that ran between 19th Avenue and Junipero Serra Boulevard. Professional offices, shops, restaurants, taverns, and the usual limited street parking.

Tamara got there a couple of minutes after five, heading west off Serra. Neither Doctor Easy's office nor the Twilight Lounge was in the first block, and that was fine, because she lucked into a parking space close to the intersection. She was wearing her coat buttoned all the way up, a scarf, and a wool cap she'd had for years and kept in the car. Not because of the weather, although it was cold and foggy out here near the ocean. Wasn't much chance Hawkins or the phony Lucas would be on the street this early, but when you were setting up a stakeout you never trusted to chance. Another lesson Bill had taught her.

She walked down toward Lagunitas, not dawdling, checking out the storefronts lining both sides of the street. The Twilight Lounge was mid-block on the south side near where the M line streetcar tracks crossed. Hawkins's office would be somewhere in the next block west, down toward 19th. Over where she was on the north side, diagonally opposite the Twilight, there was a Chinese restaurant with a window overlooking the street and tables set next to it inside. Perfect.

As early as it was, there were only two customers in the restaurant, and neither of them was sitting by the window. She claimed the table with the best view of the Twilight's entrance. A middle-aged Chinese waitress came over and Tamara ordered a pot of tea. Quarter past five now—forty-five minutes to wait. Longer, maybe a lot longer, if the phony Lucas showed up. She could linger over the tea until six, but not much past that without ordering food. Worry about that when the time came. Right now, as tense as she was, the thought of food made her stomach clench up.

Sip tea, watch the people on the street. Three men went into the Twilight Lounge, all of them white. Not too many black faces on this part of Ocean; the few that came along were easy to spot.

Five thirty.

Five forty-five.

The tea was making her feel queasy; she pushed the cup away. Here came the waitress, asking in stern tones if she wanted anything to eat. Lord. She hadn't looked at the menu, hadn't taken her eyes off the Twilight's front door. "Potstickers," she said. It was the first dish that popped into her head.

Five fifty.

She kept thinking about Lucas. If he showed, would he still be driving the five-year-old Buick? Probably. She began watching the cars that rolled by in both directions, looking for a light brown LeSabre. Dark now and hard to tell makes and colors. Streetlights, building lights, headlights helped some, but not enough. Would she recognize the Buick if it came along? Sure . . . if he hadn't had that banged-up fender fixed by now.

Five fifty-five.

And here came Deron Stewart, over on the south side. Suit,

tie, overcoat, and that swaggering walk of his. Don't overdo it, man, she thought, they'll see right through you. But then she thought, No, he'll play it right, the way he did with Hawkins on the phone. He knows his job; he won't screw up.

Stewart paused outside the lounge, adjusted his tie, and went on in.

Six.

The potstickers came. She didn't even look at the plate.

Six-oh-four.

A short black man in a trench coat came walking up from Lagunitas into her line of sight. Doctor Easy. He moved in long, quick strides, kind of a glide, straight to the Twilight's entrance and on inside.

Tamara waited, leaning forward with her hands flat on the tabletop and her face close to the window glass.

Six-oh-five.

Six ten.

"Something wrong with potstickers?"

". . . What?"

The waitress was standing next to her. "You not eating. Something wrong?"

Yes, dammit! "No," she said, and picked up one of the potstickers and bit into it. Greasy. She managed to swallow without gagging.

Six fourteen.

Damn him, she thought, he's not going to show up.

But ten seconds later, somebody else showed up.

A light-colored car swung into a slanted parking space downstreet from the Twilight, on this side, and a black man stepped out. She had a pretty good look at him and his ride both in the lights from a passing car. BMW; her lawyer sister

Claudia drove one, so Tamara knew what they looked like. He was on the heavy side, middle-aged, well dressed, his hair close-cropped. She watched him jaywalk across the street and enter the lounge.

Another of the down-low clubbers, or just a businessman wanting an after-work drink? She hadn't seen any other African Americans except Stewart go in there, but that didn't mean he and Hawkins were the only ones who patronized the place.

The restaurant was beginning to fill up, and the waitress came sidling over again. "More food?"

"Not right now."

"More tea?" The woman's tone said she'd better buy something more or get out and make room for paying customers.

"Okay. Another pot of tea."

Six thirty.

The waitress arrived with the fresh pot, set it down harder than necessary, and went away again. Tamara poured her cup full, left it untouched. Watched and waited and tried not to keep checking the time. Yeah, right. Tell yourself not to do something and you end up doing it twice as often.

Six forty-five.

Bastard definitely wasn't coming. Just Hawkins and Stewart tonight—and maybe the guy from the BMW.

Seven.

The waitress again, looking even more annoyed. The place had filled up; she didn't want a customer who hadn't ordered anything except tea and potstickers taking up space and she said so, more or less politely. Tamara didn't argue. She dredged up another Chinese dish from her memory—kung pao chicken— and the waitress went away again, satisfied.

Seven fifteen.

Tamara picked at the kung pao chicken and then, out of frustration, began shoveling it in until the plate was empty. Good-bye, diet.

Seven thirty.

Bill hated stakeouts and, man, the hate was justified. This was only the second one she'd been on, and the surroundings were a lot safer than the first time, over in the East Bay, when she'd screwed up and let that psycho kidnapper grab her. But before all the crazy stuff started happening that night, she'd been terminally bored sitting in the cramped Toyota on a dark and unfamiliar street. This was different because the case was personal, but the edge of boredom and impatience was there just the same.

How long would they sit around drinking over there? Sooner they got it done with, the sooner Stewart would call with his report and she could arrange to meet him and listen to the recording.

The wait finally ended five minutes later. Out they came— Stewart, Hawkins, and the heavyset stranger, all in a bunch. They stood talking in front of the Twilight for thirty seconds or so, then shook hands all around and went their separate ways—Hawkins down toward his office, Stewart in the opposite direction, the stranger to the curb to wait for a break in the traffic so he could cross to his Beamer.

Tamara was already on the move by then. Decided what she was going to do as soon as she saw that the heavyset guy was part of it. She tossed a ten and a five on the table and hurried out, keeping her head down as she turned upstreet. Stewart had reached his parked car, was unlocking the door; he didn't see her and she didn't try to catch his attention. Behind her, the heavyset dude had come on across the street and was taking his time with his keys.

Impulse prodded her into a loping run. At the Woodacre intersection she darted diagonally across to where she'd left the Toyota. She was inside, with the key in the ignition, when the BMW's brake lights flashed and Heavyset started to back up. Traffic kept him from getting all the way out of the space until Tamara managed to back out herself, in front of an SUV whose driver had to brake so sharply he blatted his horn at her.

A red light at 19th Avenue stopped the BMW, gave her enough time to get down there with only one car separating them. When the light changed, Heavyset turned right and the intervening car went straight, so she was right behind the Beamer when she made the swing onto 19th.

At the Sloat Boulevard intersection, he turned right again and angled over into one of the lanes that would take him onto Portola Avenue. Tamara moved into the second lane, behind another car. The BMW's rear end and taillights were distinctive enough, and the avenue well lighted enough, so she'd be able to keep him in sight from a distance.

Excitement bubbled in her. This was more like it! Following somebody in the dark, trying to keep pace . . . there was a thrill in that kind of thing. Not a dangerous thrill like that time in San Leandro; a small and relatively safe one. Mostly her job consisted of putting in a lot of desk time at the agency, combing the Net, answering phones, compiling reports. Monotonous after a while. Fieldwork now and then, even on a grim mission like this one, was a sure cure for boredom. She'd intended to do it more often, but there never seemed to be enough time. From now on she'd make the time.

The Beamer headed straight up Portola, not fast and not slow. No problem keeping pace. A red light stopped them both at Claremont. And while she was waiting for it to change, the ringtone on her cell phone began chirping.

She got it out of her purse, switched on before the light turned green. Deron Stewart. "Zeller was a no-show," he said.

"I know. I was across the street the whole time you were in the lounge."

". . . Didn't tell me you'd be there."

"My business," she said. "Who was the heavyset guy came in a few minutes late?"

He said, "Sharp eye," which she supposed was meant as a compliment for her observational skills. "His name's Roland."

"First or last name?"

"Just Roland. That's all he'd give."

"One of the down lows?"

"Yeah. Wouldn't say what he does for a living, either. Didn't say much at all, just sat there listening and checking me out. But he lives here in the city. Hawkins referred to him once as a neighbor."

The BMW had passed through the O'Shaugnessy intersection at the top of Twin Peaks and they were moving downhill on the far side. The light at the turnoff for Diamond Heights Boulevard was green; the Beamer went right on through, onto the winding stretch of Upper Market. Wherever the heavyset dude, Roland, was headed, it wasn't straight home. Hawkins lived in Monterey Heights, on the edge of St. Francis Wood, and now that section was behind them to the southwest.

Stewart said, "You still on, Tamara?"

"Still on. Did Hawkins or Roland mention Zeller at all?"

"Not until I brought up his name."

"And?"

"He's still in the city, I got that much out of Hawkins, but not where he's living or what he's doing. One thing: the three of them are involved in a business deal."

"What kind of business deal?"

"Something to do with a fund that helps needy black families. Easy asked Roland if he was going ahead; Roland said he thought so, as long as Easy and Zeller were still on board, but there had to be another reading before he'd be convinced."

"Reading?"

"Your guess is as good as mine. That was all either of them would say."

"So they didn't try to involve you in this deal."

"No. And I didn't want to make them suspicious by pushing it."

"You pass with them all right?"

"Must have, as far as the club goes. Got myself invited to their next meeting."

"When?"

"Saturday night. Eight o'clock at the SoMa loft. Want the address now?"

"Later. Zeller going to be there?"

"Likely. Their regular group, Hawkins said."

At Castro, Roland swung over into the left-turn lane for Divisadero and caught the light just before it turned yellow. Tamara had to jump a lane, cutting off another car, and lay down a heavy foot to make it across the intersection before the oncoming traffic started moving.

Stewart said, "I got everything on the voice recorder. You want it tonight or wait until tomorrow?"

"Tonight."

"Tell me where you live and I'll drop it off."

Talking to him, driving one-handed, had become a distraction. Besides, it was illegal now to use a cell phone while driving; if a cop spotted her she'd probably get pulled over. She said, "I'll get back to you in a few minutes—I'm in the middle of something now," and clicked off.

Straight along Divisadero to Oak, right turn, west four blocks to Fillmore, left turn on Fillmore. The Western Addition, one of the few neighborhoods that had survived the 1906 earthquake, once a black ghetto but integrated and Yuppified now. After a couple of blocks the Beamer slowed, eased over into the right lane. Tamara did the same, hanging back. Small businesses and apartment buildings strung out along there, most of the businesses closed.

In mid-block, brake lights flashed crimson and the BMW came to a quick stop. Getting set to park, and in the only available space. She had no choice but to swing around into the inside lane.

There was a bus stop on the corner; she cut over into it. In the rearview mirror she could see the Beamer backing up into the space. She shut off the headlights but not the engine. Roland finished his park job and the BMW went dark; she watched his big shape get out, circle around the front onto the sidewalk. He stood there for a couple of seconds, doing something with his coat, and then moved upstreet about fifty yards before stopping again at one of the dimly lighted storefronts. So what was he doing, window-shopping?

No. He stepped forward, disappeared inside.

Tamara stayed where she was, watching, for five minutes. Roland didn't come back out.

A Muni bus was headed her way; she put the headlights on, drove around the corner. No parking spaces. Circled the block—still no spaces—and came back slow on Fillmore. Most of the stores looked closed, but several showed night lights and she wasn't real sure which one Roland had gone into.

She pulled into the bus zone again. Leave the car here for a couple of minutes, she thought, not much of a ticket risk now. She got out the notepad and pen she kept in her purse, then walked quickly to Roland's Beamer. When the street was clear she stepped out in front to peer at the license plate. 5XZX994. She scribbled the number on the pad before she moved on up the sidewalk to check the storefronts.

Barbecue take-out restaurant, dry cleaners, card shop—all connected parts of a single building, all closed now. A row of apartments made up the building's second story. The storefront next to the card shop showed light through a gap between wine-colored curtains drawn across its front window; lights were on in the apartment above it, too. Propped between the curtains and the window glass was a large printed placard. Tamara eased up close enough to read the lettering.

PSYCHIC READINGS BY ALISHA
Palm   Tarot

Yes!

This was the place Roland had disappeared into, all right. Tamara risked a quick peek through the lighted gap. All she could see was part of a sparsely furnished room, a table with a red-shaded lamp on it, more dark red curtains drawn over a doorway at the rear. No sign of Roland, no sign of Alisha.

But Tamara didn't need to see the woman to know who she was. Alisha was Mama's name. Roland had led her straight to Mama.

And where Mama was, her miserable son was sure to be nearby.

12

TAMARA

She called Deron Stewart back and arranged to meet him on South Park, outside the agency. Seemed like the best place; she didn't want him coming to her apartment on Potrero Hill, and anywhere else, even a neutral public spot, thinned out the strictly business atmosphere she'd established with him. Last thing she needed tonight was him hitting on her.

All the way to South Park, she felt a grim elation. So Mama was a psychic. Or pretending to be one. There were plenty of honest card and palm readers in the city, but Tamara would bet her bank account that Alisha wasn't one of them. Not with a down-low thief for a son.

And what about Lucas? Was he still living with Mama—in that apartment above the psychic shop, maybe?

If he was living there, he'd be keeping a low profile. Real low, if he and Mama were setting up a scam and he'd been the one to steer Roland, a believer who trusted to "readings" before he acted on important matters, to Alisha. Made sense that way. This investment fund Roland and Doctor Easy were involved in figured to be the scam; Lucas had told James his business was "investments." A con designed to bilk cash out of at least two and maybe the rest of the down-low clubbers. A score big enough to warrant weeks of setup and expense—the kind of score small-time grifters dream about.

Tamara didn't need psychic powers to know she was reading it right, or close to right. It explained everything, including why Lucas and Alisha were still hanging on in San Francisco. Make the big score and then vanish—poof!—to someplace thousands of miles away before any of the vics knew what'd hit them.

She parked the Toyota in the South Park garage, waited for Stewart in the little park across the street from the agency's building. Restaurants, a couple of clubs in the area, so there were people around and music throbbing in the cold night. Funny, but as she stood there by the playground, the elation she'd felt earlier drained away and left her feeling edgy. Celebration was premature. Still a lot to do, still things that could go wrong.

Stewart finally came hurrying from the direction of 3rd Street. "Sorry it took me so long," he said. "Couldn't find a parking place."

She made herself say, "No problem."

"Cold out here. How about we go up to your office?"

"Not necessary. This won't take long. The tape?"

"You want the recorder, too?"

"Just the tape, unless it won't play in a Sony digital."

"It'll play. Sony's what I've got." He brought the recorder out of his coat pocket, removed and handed her the tape. "I played a little of it back," he said. "The lounge was noisy, but you can hear most of what we said pretty clearly."

"When did Roland and Hawkins talk about the deal they're in with Zeller? What point on the tape?"

"Toward the end. As we were getting ready to leave. I picked up the check, by the way. Figured I should."

"Put it on the expense account."

"I will," he said. "I take it you want me to go to the club meeting in SoMa Saturday night?"

"Probably, if you can keep from having sex with one of them."

He laughed. "Cost you extra if I can't."

Tamara just looked at him.

"Okay, not funny. Sorry. Don't worry; I can handle it."

"I wasn't worried," she said. "What's the SoMa address?"

"One-eight-seven-seven-nine Harrison. Top-floor loft, Unit Six. You figure on being there?"

"I don't know yet. See what happens between now and Saturday."

"If you do want me to go and Zeller shows, I could find a way to slip out and give you a quick call, let you know. And then see what I can find out about him—where he lives, what he's doing for his bread."

"And get him talking about his mother, if you can."

"His mother? Why?"

Tamara stonewalled the question.

Stewart shrugged and said, "Okay. What's her name?"

"Alisha. But you're not supposed to know that."

"Anything else?"

"If there's any relationship between him and Roland, aside from the club thing."

Stewart nodded. "You want the whole evening recorded, all the sports rap?"

"No need. Just anything that's relevant to Zeller, his mother, Roland."

"You got it." He shoved his hands in his coat pockets, said, "Be seeing you," and went away toward 3rd at a fast walk.

Tamara crossed the street, unlocked the front door to the building, and climbed the stairs to the agency offices. Stewart had been thoroughly professional tonight, except for that one wisecrack; hadn't come on to her at all. Good. Fine. And yet, in spite of herself, she couldn't help feeling a vague disappointment. The man was a hound and the only women hounds didn't bother to hit on were the ones nobody wanted, the skanks and woofers. A tacit rejection to make her feel unattractive and undesirable . . .

Pathetic.

Don't start trippin' on yourself, girl!

In her office, the first thing she did was to boot up her Mac and check on Psychic Readings by Alisha. There was a listing in the current city directory; Tamara made a note of the phone number. No Web site, no other Net reference. City treasurer and tax collector's office next. No Business Registration Certificate. And no application for a New Business Permit on file.

So Mama hadn't been operating here for long. Three months max, that was about as long as you could get away without applying for a business license in San Francisco before you got caught. One more strike against Alisha. One more reason to believe she was into a bigger scam than phony psychic readings.

Tamara ran the Fillmore Street address to find out who owned the building. Eldon Management Company. Thomas Eldon, president. Address on Sutter Street downtown. Eldon Management owned three contiguous buildings on that block of Fillmore, in fact, but none of the tenants' names was listed. Tomorrow she'd try to pry Alisha's last name out of Thomas Eldon or one of his representatives, and at that it probably wouldn't be her real name. Good bet that she'd paid her deposit and rent in cash and that the management company, like a lot of them, wasn't too scrupulous about making background checks.

Something else that would have to wait until the morning: finding out who Roland was. State law forbid licensed detective agencies from running direct DMV license searches to get the names and addresses of registered car owners. She had a contact in the bureau who'd do it for her, but only during business hours.

Time for Stewart's tape. She plugged it into her Sony digital, fast-forwarded to near the end, ran it back and forth until she found the exchange he'd told her about. Lots of background noise, as Stewart had said, but with the volume turned all the way up the men's voices were clear enough—Roland's was a deep baritone—and you could understand all but a few words here and there.

Doctor Easy: Before we leave, Roland . . . have you made a decision yet?

Roland: About the fund? I think I'm ready to go ahead, as long as you and Lucas are still on board.

Doctor Easy: We are. It's a solid investment, seems to me. And a worthwhile cause.

Roland: No question about that.

Doctor Easy: You still sound hesitant.

Roland: I'm not, but [I? Vi?] . . . completely convinced yet.

Doctor Easy: Another reading?

Roland: Yes.

Doctor Easy: Will you know by Saturday night?

Roland: I think so.

Doctor Easy: Good. Lucas is anxious to get things moving.

Stewart: What sort of investment, if you don't mind my asking?

Doctor Easy: You'll meet Lucas tomorrow night. He'll give you the details if you're interested.

Stewart: You said it was a worthwhile cause?

Doctor Easy: Worthwhile, and potentially lucrative for the investors. Helping black families in need.

Stewart: Helping them how?

Doctor Easy: Tomorrow night, Deron. Let's be moving on now. I'm late for dinner as it is.

Investment fund to help black families in need. Worthwhile, lucrative—the perfect con to work on well-off African Americans who were both socially conscious and greedy. Uh-huh. Scam devised by Lucas, probably with Mama's help. Manipulate the vics by pretending to be one of the investors himself. Roland needs more convincing than Doctor Easy, but he's into psychics, Lucas introduces him to Mama, and she tells him it's a terrific deal and he should go for it. One more reading—yeah. Chances are he's the big pigeon, with the most money to invest; that's why they've spent so much time and effort setting him up.

Tamara listened to the section again, and a third time, trying to make out the words Roland had said right before "completely convinced." Somebody had called out for the bartender at that point. First word: "Vi," not "I." She was pretty sure of that now. The other missing word. "Isn't?" Had to be.

"Vi isn't completely convinced yet."

Vi. Short for what? Violet, Viola, Vivian . . . and a bunch

of other possibilities. Whatever, she must be Roland's wife. So were they both into psychics? Or maybe just her and she was the one who needed convincing by Alisha's readings? But if that was it, then why had Roland gone straight to Mama's from the lounge meeting tonight?

Lots of questions that needed answering before she could figure out the best way to blow up the scheme. She had to have evidence, too, in order to put Lucas and Alisha away. Didn't exist anymore where the identity and property theft was concerned; and using somebody's name wasn't a crime, unless you did it to commit fraud. But setting up a scam wasn't a fraud felony until and unless money changed hands. And if you waited too long after that happened, they'd skip and disappear with the loot.

Tamara listened to the entire tape, start to finish, in case there was anything useful Stewart might've missed. There wasn't. Most of the conversation was feeler stuff, strangers getting to know one another in general ways, and sports chatter. Doctor Easy did most of the talking, asking Stewart questions, some of them with thinly veiled sexual overtones. Stewart fielded them all smoothly and with just the right amount of nervousness, the way he had on the phone with Hawkins. Roland, as Stewart had told her, didn't have much to say. A listener, she thought. Brought along to evaluate the new recruit. At some point Roland had probably given Doctor Easy a signal to go ahead and issue the invitation to the club meeting tomorrow night.

Zeller was mentioned a few times, mostly by Stewart in casual attempts to draw out information. No such luck. The brief exchange about the investment fund was all there was on that subject.

It was late, after ten o'clock, when she switched off the

recorder and locked the tape in her desk drawer. She was tired, gritty eyed, but she doubted she'd sleep much again tonight. Too keyed up.

Quiet in the office, too—too quiet. That late-night stillness empty buildings had. The walls were thick enough and insulated enough so that none of the South Park sounds penetrated. She was in the midst of a big, teeming city, with only a hundred yards or so separating her from crowds of people having a good time, but it was as if she were a long way off from anybody, alone on an island of light surrounded by darkness.

Lucas had done this to her. Just when she'd gotten her life back in sync, he'd screwed it up again. Brought the loneliness back. Damn him! Then she thought: Sure, blame him, but blame yourself, too. Tamara Corbin, hotshot de-tective, who makes all the wrong personal decisions, who tries to live in the fast lane but keeps ending up as lifestyle roadkill.

She got herself out of there. She had a weird feeling that if she stayed any longer, she might *really* start feeling sorry for herself.

13

I was two minutes from home, coming down off Diamond Heights on my way to the agency, when my cell phone went off. Never fails. Seems like the thing is always silent until I'm in the car and driving and then it rings incessantly. Early start today. It was only eight fifteen.

I could have let the call go onto voice mail, but I'm compulsive about answering the phone—a habit I picked up in the lean days when I first opened the agency and couldn't afford to miss a potential client. I pulled over and stopped before I answered, something else I'm compulsive about. People who drive with a cell clapped against their ear and too-little attention to the road are one of my pet peeves. You don't see quite as many doing it now that the new state law banning hand-held cellular phones while operating a motor vehicle finally has kicked in, but there're still too many to suit me. The fines aren't nearly stiff enough to be an effective deterrent, and the ones who risk getting caught seem to take a sneaky self-satisfaction in flaunting a law they consider an unnecessary infringement on their personal rights. If I were a patrol cop, I'd spend a couple of days a week pulling them over and writing them up just to hear them whine.

The caller was Helen Alvarez. Excited and a little breathless. "It happened again last night," she said.

"What did?"

"He broke into Margaret's house again. Patterson or whoever he is. Walked right into her bedroom at three a.m., bold as brass."

"He didn't harm her?"

"No. Just scared the wits out of her."

"She all right now?"

"Better than most women her age would be."

"Did she get a good look at him?"

"No. Wouldn't have even if all the lights had been on."

"Why not?"

"He was wearing a sheet."

"He was . . . what?"

"A sheet," Helen Alvarez said grimly, "wearing a white sheet and making noises like a ghost."

When I got to the Abbott house I found a reception committee of three on the front porch: Helen Alvarez, Leonard Crenshaw, and Everett Belasco, talking animatedly among themselves. Crenshaw was saying as I came up the walk, ". . . Should have called the police instead. They're the ones ought to be investigating this."

"What can they do?" his sister said. "There aren't any signs of breaking and entering this time, either. Nothing damaged, nothing stolen. Just Margaret's word that a man in a sheet was there in the first place. They'd probably say she imagined the whole thing."

"Well, maybe she did," Belasco said. "I mean, all that nonsense about her dead husband coming back to haunt her . . ."

"Ev, she didn't say it was a ghost she saw. She said it was a man in a sheet pretending to be a ghost. There's a big difference."

"She still could've imagined it. Or dreamed it."

Mrs. Alvarez appealed to me. "It happened; I'm sure it did. She may be a bit fanciful, but she doesn't see things that aren't there."

"Is she up to talking about it?"

"I told her you were coming. She's waiting."

"Guess you don't need me," Belasco said. He bumped against Crenshaw as he turned, winced, and rubbed at a bandage across the back of his right hand.

Crenshaw asked, "What'd you do to your hand, Ev?"

"Goddamn knife slipped while I was slicing bacon this morning. Hurts like the devil."

"If it's a deep cut," Mrs. Alvarez said, "you better have a doctor look at it."

"No, it's not deep. Just painful." A gust of icy wind swept over the porch. Belasco shivered and said, "Damn, it's cold out here. Come on, Leonard, I've got a pot of fresh coffee made."

"No thanks," Crenshaw said, "I got work to do." He gave me a brief disapproving look and said pointedly to his sister, "Just remember, Helen—chickens always come home to roost."

"Yes, and you can't make an omelette without breaking eggs."

"Bah," he said.

"Silly old fool," she said.

Mrs. Alvarez and I went into the house. Margaret Abbott was perched on her Boston rocker, a shawl over her lap and Spike, the orange tabby, curled up asleep on the shawl. She looked tired; the rouge she'd applied to her cheeks was like bloody splotches on too-white parchment. Still, she seemed in good spirits. And she showed no reluctance to discuss her latest ordeal.

"It's really rather amusing," she said, "now that I look back on it. A grown man wearing a sheet and moaning and groaning like Casper with a tummy ache."

"You're sure it was a man?"

"Oh yes. Definitely a man."

"You didn't recognize his voice?"

"Well, he didn't speak. Just moaned and groaned."

"Did you say anything to him?"

"I believe I asked what he thought he was doing in my bedroom. Yes, and I said that he'd better not have harmed Spike. It was Spike crying that woke me, you see."

"Not the intruder coming into your bedroom?"

"No. Spike yowling as if he'd been hurt. He must have heard the man come into the house and gone to investigate and the man stepped on him or kicked him. Poor Spike. You've been through so much, haven't you, dear?"

Spike opened one eye and yawned.

I said, "Then what happened, Mrs. Abbott? After you woke up."

"Well, I saw a flickery sort of light in the hallway. At first I couldn't imagine what it was."

"Flashlight," Mrs. Alvarez said.

"Yes. It came closer, into the doorway, then switched off and the man walked right up to the foot of my bed and began moaning and groaning and jumping around." She smiled wanly. "Really, it was rather funny."

"How long did he keep up his act?"

"Not long. Just until I spoke sternly to him."

"Then he ran out?"

"Still moaning and groaning, yes. I suppose he wanted me to think he was the spirit of my late husband. As if I wouldn't know a living man from a dead one. Or Carl, in or out of a sheet."

Charley Doyle, I was thinking. A stupid ghost stunt was just the sort a pea-brain like him would come up with. He'd deny it, of course. And probably claim he'd spent all of last night with darlin' Melanie, not that that was a stand-up alibi; she would lie for him just as readily as she drank and slept with him. But I'd have a talk with him just the same. Maybe, if I handled him right, I could rattle his cage enough to make him incriminate himself.

I called Dependable Glass Service. Doyle was out on a job, due back this time before noon and not scheduled to go out again until after the lunch hour. Okay. It was a little after ten now. That gave me time to swing by the agency.

Tamara was busy when I got there, simultaneously talking on the phone and thumping on her computer keyboard. I waited until she finished with the call before I went into her office.

"Got something for you to do when you have time," I said.

She said, "Doesn't everybody," but she didn't sound grouchy today. Tired and a little distracted but in a reasonably good mood.

"Run a check for me. Whitney Middle School's enrollment. See if you can find out who belongs to the initials *Z.U.*"

"What case is that for?"

"No case. Personal."

She made a note of what I'd asked for. Then, "Whitney Middle School? Isn't that the one Emily goes to?"

"Yes."

"Something to do with her?"

"I'd rather not discuss it right now. Any more than you want to discuss what's been bothering you lately."

"Uh-huh," she said. "How important?"

"Pretty important. But you don't have to drop everything else to do it. Sometime today."

"No problem. If I come up with a name for Z.U., you want a full package on whoever it is?"

"As much as you can get. Address, parentage, school record, ever in trouble of any kind."

She nodded and went back to tapping on the keyboard. The printer on her workstation thumped and began to ratchet a printout.

Dismissed.

Charley Doyle was not happy to see me. He was sitting in his pickup in Dependable's side yard, eating a sandwich that had both mayonnaise and mustard in it; I knew that because of the yellow-white smear on one side of his mouth. He scowled at me through the open driver's window.

"You again," he said.

"Me again."

"Now what you want? I told you last time—"

"There was another incident at your aunt's last night."

"Incident? What the hell you mean, incident?"

"Another home invasion. Intruder at three a.m. dressed up in a sheet and making noises like a ghost."

". . . You kidding me?"

"Do I sound like I'm kidding?"

"She okay? Auntie?"

"Fine. She scared him off."

"Scared him? How?"

"She's a tough old lady. She doesn't really believe in ghosts."

Doyle grunted, looked at his sandwich, took another bite out of it; the bite and the way he chewed indicated he was angry, whether at me, his aunt, or the home invasion I couldn't tell.

"Where were you last night, Mr. Doyle?"

"Me? Christ, you think I'm the guy? Bust into my aunt's place dressed up in a fuckin' sheet?"

"I asked you a question, that's all."

"Yeah, sure. Well, it wasn't me. I was with my woman all night, at her place."

"Melanie."

"Yeah, Melanie. All night. Ask her, you don't believe me."

"Maybe I'll do that."

"Goddamn snoop," he said. "Coming around where I work, accusing me. If you wasn't an old man, I'd push your face in."

"Welcome to try anyway. Assault is a bigger crime than malicious mischief."

"Fuck your mischief," he said cleverly. He dumped the rest of his sandwich into a paper sack on the seat beside him. "Now I lost my appetite."

"That's too bad. I'll bet your aunt lost hers, too."

Doyle opened the truck's door and climbed out. I backed up a step to give him room—just the one step, so he wouldn't get the idea I was retreating from him. But he had no intention of following up on his threat to push my face in. He stood flat-footed, glaring at me out of his little piggish eyes.

"Listen," he said. "I told you before, I didn't have nothing to do with what's been going on at her place, that ghost crap and the rest."

"That's right," I said. "You did mention ghosts the other day, didn't you."

"Huh?"

" 'Her dead-husband's friggin' ghost,' I think you said. How'd you know?"

"Huh?"

"That your aunt had a fanciful notion about Carl visiting her from the Other Side."

". . . What the hell you talkin' about?"

"The notion only came to her three days ago. You said you hadn't seen or talked to her for some time before that. So how'd you know about it?"

"I, uh . . ." Doyle's blocky face had developed a burgundy flush. "Wasn't just two days ago she started in about ghosts. She said it to me the last time I seen her."

"Did she? I'll ask her about that."

"You don't ask her nothing. Stay away from her."

"I can't do that."

"I don't have to tell you nothing, you hear? I don't have to talk to you no more at all."

"Not to me, maybe. How about the police?"

The piggish eyes narrowed. He made a fist and waved it in my direction, not too close. I knew what was coming next. When guys like him are stuck for answers or caught out on something or other, they quit what passes for thinking and go straight to belligerent anger.

"I had enough of your bullshit," he said. "You leave me alone from now on, man. Don't come around bugging me no more. You do and I'll bust you up good, old bastard or not."

I showed him my wolf's smile, to see if it would have any effect on him. The madder they get, the more likely they are to let something slip. Not Doyle, though. He fixed me with a black look and then stalked past me, not quite touching me on the way, and disappeared inside Dependable Glass's warehouse.

I went and sat in my car, with my hands resting on the wheel. And then I just sat, staring, while things happened inside my head—plunk, plunk, plunk, like pinballs dropping into holes and slots.

Well, hell, I thought.

Getting old, all right. And real slow on the uptake.

14

TAMARA

She'd been in better spirits come morning. The feelings of loneliness and isolation were night creatures that crawled away in the daylight and left her focused again on Lucas and Alisha.

The first thing she'd done was drive over to the Western Addition. Scouting mission this time. Figure Lucas was living with Mama in that apartment above Psychic Readings by Alisha; figure he still drove that light brown Buick LeSabre. Then chances were, it'd be parked somewhere in the vicinity. Private garages cost a bundle in the city, public lots weren't cheap, either, and it'd be costing him and Mama enough as it was to live and work their con. So it had to be street parking whenever he was in the neighborhood.

She'd thought of this last night, but driving around and trying to pick out a light brown Buick in the dark didn't make much sense. Lot easier to identify colors and models in daylight. There wouldn't be many brown Buick LeSabres parked in that neighborhood, and only one with a scrape and dent on the right front fender.

Turned out there weren't any.

She drove around there for an hour, roaming two and three times over every street within a six-block radius of the Fillmore address. Just one Buick compact and it was white, not light brown, and it didn't have any fender dents.

Bust.

She consoled herself with the thought that maybe she'd just missed him; maybe he'd gotten up as early as she had and gone off on some business or other. Worth coming back again, unless she turned up a better lead in the meantime. Even if Lucas wasn't living with Mama, he'd come visit her at some point, wouldn't he? Sooner or later she was bound to get lucky.

Alisha's last name was Jones.

And she was Jamaican.

Sure. Right. And the Pope was Jewish and the oil companies cared deeply about the environment and true love was waiting for Tamara just around the corner.

At 10:00 a.m., when Eldon Management Company opened for business, she called them up and identified herself as a representative of the city treasurer and tax collector's office. Every now and then when you used a ploy like that, the person you talked to was leery enough to ask for a callback number and you had to either improvise or blow it off. Usually it worked with no hassle, though, and it did this time; the nasal-voiced woman at Eldon didn't question Tamara when she fed out her line: calling because it had come to the office's attention that one of the company's Fillmore Street tenants had failed to apply for a business license. Information, please, on the proprietor of Psychic Readings by Alisha.

Alisha Jones. Jamaican by birth, immigrated to the United

States two years ago. Occupied the space, which also had a small apartment at the rear, for the past three months on a one-year lease. Paid first and last month's rent in cash. Was anyone else's name on the lease? No. Had Eldon checked Alisha Jones's references or examined her green card? The woman hemmed and hawed and finally admitted that they "hadn't found it necessary" to do either one. Did they have any other information on their tenant, such as a relative who might be living with her? Sorry, no, they didn't.

The woman asked then if Eldon should take action against Ms. Jones for her noncompliance with the city's business practice laws. Tamara said, "No, don't say anything to Ms. Jones. We'll contact her directly," and managed not to bang the receiver down.

Running a search on Alisha Jones would be a waste of time. Too many Joneses in the world, even if by some miracle that was Mama's real name. Instead Tamara called Marjorie, the agency's contact at the DMV, gave her the BMW's license plate number. Ten minutes later she had the name and address of the registered owner.

Which wasn't anybody named Roland. Or even a man.

Viveca Adams Inman, 4719 North Point, San Francisco.

Viveca—Vi for short.

Married to Roland? Back on the Net to find out. And the answer was no.

Widow of Jason K. Inman, who'd made a pile of bucks in the marine salvage business and died four years ago of complications from gallbladder surgery, age fifty-five. No children. Her age now: forty-one. And judging from her address, she'd inherited a nice piece of city real estate close to the Marina Green and the yacht harbor.

She was also white.

So what was a black switch-hitter named Roland doing driving a Beamer registered in her name? Friend? Neighbor? Lover? How about chauffeur or trusty black gofer?

Tamara sifted through the Google hits on Viveca Inman. Most were mentions of her in connection with her husband; those since his death were mostly from *Chronicle* social columns. Arts patron, regular at social and charity events, hosted this or that dinner party. One brief mention of interest, a little over a year ago: with the aid of a "psychic consultation" she'd decided to authorize the writing and publication of a university press book about her husband and his salvage operations. So were Vi and Roland both into psychics? Could be Inman was a potential investor, too, and she was the one who needed "another reading" before making up her mind. Her charity work and dependance on psychics fit that explanation.

What didn't fit anywhere yet was Roland.

Here and there in the columns men were mentioned—"Mrs. Inman was escorted by So-and-So," like that—but Roland wasn't one of them. Not his real name—an alias he used to hide his identity from new down-low club recruits? Could also be he kept a low profile for reasons of his own, or because of the racial difference. Or maybe he *was* a trusted employee after all, permitted to use the Beamer on his days off. Looks could be deceiving; Tamara knew that if anybody did. So could intelligent-sounding voices and nice clothes and a smooth line.

Next step? The obvious was to call up Viveca Inman on some pretext or other and ask about Roland straight out, but Tamara couldn't think of one that didn't sound contrived and the last thing she wanted was to arouse suspicion. One other possibility occurred to her: Joe DeFalco, Bill's buddy who worked as a reporter and feature writer for the *Chronicle*.

She got DeFalco on the phone, told him briefly what she needed. Naturally he wanted to know why she was interested in Viveca Inman. The man was always looking for a story, something that would help him make a bigger name for himself. An old-fashioned muckraker, Bill called him, with a yen for a Pulitzer Prize that he'd never get.

Nothing juicy or newsworthy, she told him, just an insurance case the agency was working on that didn't involve Inman directly. No lie there. He said, well, if it turned into anything important, she'd better let him know or he wouldn't do any more favors for her or her partner. She said okay, and DeFalco said okay, he'd talk to the paper's society editor and get back to her ASAP.

While she waited, Tamara ran the b.g. search Jake had asked for on the East Bay trucker, Bud Linkhauser. Easy job. She was just wrapping it up when DeFalco called back.

"I don't have much for you," he said. "Nobody named Roland in Inman's life, at least not for public consumption. If there was, Isabel'd know it."

"Men in her life, black or white?"

"Lots of men. Very popular lady. Money and good looks equal a long line of sniffers in the social set."

"Yes, but does she date black men?"

"Isabel says no. Strictly white on white."

"Black neighbors?"

"In the Marina within spitting distance of the yacht club? Don't you wish."

"What about African American employees?"

"Again, no," DeFalco said. "And if your next question is, is she prejudiced against blacks, that's another no. One of her charities is an adoption program for crack babies born in the ghettos."

Score one for Viveca Inman. "But she is into psychics?"

"In a big way. Consults regularly, won't make any major decisions without getting her cards read and fortune told." He let loose a derisive snorting sound that resonated like a fart. "A load of crap, if you ask me. Psychics are in the same class with mediums, astrologers, gypsy fortune-tellers."

"Lot of people believe in them."

"A lot of people believe the government has our best interests at heart, too. One of these days I'm going to write an exposé."

"On psychics or the government?"

"Hell," he said, "both."

"Any particular psychic Inman sees?"

"Different ones, probably compares readings."

Tamara asked, "Close women friends I can talk to?"

"Isabel says her best friend is Tricia Dupont. Another rich widow big into charity work."

"Tricia Dupont. *D-u-p-o-n-t?*"

"Right. Lives in Sea Cliff. But if you want to talk to her today, you can reach her at the Senior Center at Aquatic Park. She does volunteer work with the senior literacy program one day a week and this is it."

"Anybody else I can talk to?"

DeFalco gave her two other names, both women. Then he said, "Don't forget, Tamara. If there's anything worth a story in this case of yours, you let me know right away."

"Count on it."

He made the farting noise again and broke the connection.

T alking to Tricia Dupont in person was better than trying to pry information out of a stranger over the phone. A call to the Senior Center got Tamara a reluctant appointment for ten minutes of the woman's time, but not until twelve forty-five. That gave her time to make another pass around the Western Addition neighborhood.

Still no light brown Buick LeSabre, with or without scrapes and dents.

T he San Francisco Senior Center at Aquatic Park was in the old ship-shaped Maritime Museum at the western end of Fisherman's Wharf. Nice location when the weather was good; lawn, beach, the long Municipal Pier that jutted out into the bay were right across a driveway and parking area behind the building. Not so nice today. The wind that came whipping in off the water was meat-locker cold, creating rippling whitecaps on the bay's gray surface. Terrific. Tricia Dupont hadn't wanted to meet inside the Center but outside on the stadium-like bleacher seats that stretched above the strip of sandy beach where the whack jobs who pleasure-swam in the frigid bay waters congregated. Freeze her ass off out there.

Mrs. Dupont was in her late forties, tucked and Botoxed, dark haired under a cloth cap and no doubt a lot warmer in an expensive lamb's wool coat than Tamara was in her down jacket. First thing Mrs. Dupont said after they shook hands was, "You're a private investigator, Ms. Corbin?" She sounded a little dubious. Not because I'm a black woman, Tamara thought wryly, because I'm a *young* black woman.

"That's right." She proved it by showing her creds.

"And the case you're investigating involves Viveca Inman?"

"Not exactly. If she's involved at all, it's indirectly and without her knowledge."

"I see," Mrs. Dupont said, still dubious. "But why come to me? Why not talk to Mrs. Inman? Or have you done that already?"

"Not yet. I need more information first."

"Which you believe she won't give you. Is that it?"

"I'm trying to save her some grief, Mrs. Dupont. But I can't do that without more evidence than I have right now."

"I don't understand. What kind of grief?"

"Do you know anything about a charity designed to help black families in need? One she's thinking of investing in?"

"No, I . . . Oh, wait, yes. The O.S. Fund."

"O.S.?"

"Operation Save. Vi was looking into it as a possible investment."

"What can you tell me about this fund?"

"Not very much. She didn't go into details. Is there something wrong with it? Is that what you're investigating?"

"Partly. Roland the one who suggested she invest in it?"

". . . Who?"

"Roland. Friend or acquaintance of Mrs. Inman's."

"I'm sorry, I don't know anyone by that name."

"African American, heavyset, good-looking, about fifty."

"Well, that might be anyone. Vi is very active in the black community."

"She knows him well enough to let him use her car."

"Her car? Which car?"

"Silver BMW. He was driving it last night."

"Ah, the Beamer. She must have sold it then."

"Sold it?"

"She just bought a new Ferrari. She also has a Mercedes—she doesn't need three cars."

Who does? Tamara thought.

"Alfred," Mrs. Dupont said.

"Excuse me?"

"Yes, of course, that's who it must be. She mentioned he was interested in the Beamer."

"Who would Alfred be?"

"Alfred Mantle. If he did buy the Beamer, he's the man you're looking for—he fits your description. I've never heard him called Roland, but I suppose that could be his middle name."

"What's his relationship with Mrs. Inman?"

"Professional. He's one of the attorneys who handled her late husband's business affairs."

"For which firm?"

"Lynch, Fosberg, Snyder, and Lynch. But he's no longer with them, of course."

"Why 'of course'?"

"He was appointed to the bench two years ago. He's a Unified Family Court judge now."

Tamara took that in. And pretty soon she was smiling, slow and sardonic.

"Is something amusing, Ms. Corbin?"

"No. Just thinking of something somebody told me."

James, quoting Lucas: *Said the other guys were professional people or businessmen, all married men and none of 'em judgmental. Then he laughed like something was funny. Said, well, except one man who was but wouldn't be. . . . Fuckin' double-talk.*

Uh-uh, not double-talk at all. Lucas's idea of a clever joke. He hadn't meant "judgmental."

He'd meant Judge Mantle.

When she got back to the agency, she ran a check on Operation Save. They had a Web site, but there was no other information on the fund—and she went in pretty deep on the search.

According to the Web site, Operation Save was a charitable investment fund designed to help black home owners get current on their mortgage payments in order to prevent foreclosure. There were a lot of testimonials from people in various cities in California and photographs of homes that'd been "saved," plus offers of prospectuses and additional info. E-mail link, but no street address or telephone number. On the surface it all seemed straightforward and aboveboard—the soft-sell kind of charity that played on the "help your brothers and sisters in their time of need" theme. But if it was legitimate, why wasn't there any more available information?

It smelled like a scam to her.

Anybody could set up a Web site loaded with photographs and testimonials and brotherhood BS. Smoke screen to help rope in the marks. It was just the kind of con a couple of no-conscience grifters would come up with. Nasty. Preying on African Americans with cash in the bank and a streak of altruism mixed in with their hunger for more. And the pretense of helping black folks who genuinely needed bailout money made it even worse. One of Ma's friends in Redwood City had lost her house to bank foreclosure and so had an S.F. couple sister Claudia knew—African Americans who'd finally gotten a piece of the American Dream, thanks to relaxed credit standards, only to lose it again when the whole mortgage thing blew up and the economy went into the toilet.

But Lucas and Mama didn't care about any of that. Hell, no. The proliferation of loan defaults by brothers and sisters was nothing more to that pair than the setup basis for a big con, the score of a lifetime.

Only it wasn't going to happen.

No way would she let it happen.

15

JAKE RUNYON

He spent his morning interviewing residents of the Valencia Street apartment where Troy Madison and Jennifer Piper lived, trying to get a line on either or both of them. Margaret Adams, the woman who'd overheard them leaving, was home today, but all she had to tell him that he didn't already know was that Madison had said something on the way out of the building about "a short trip, for now." So maybe they hadn't been planning to run far, at least not that night. There was a good chance they were still somewhere in the greater Bay Area.

He'd had his cellular switched off during the interviews, as he always did except when he was expecting an important call. When he left the building, his voice mail yielded two messages, one from Tamara and the other from Coy Madison.

Runyon called the agency first. Nothing urgent; Tamara had the background data on Bud Linkhauser that he'd requested. Except for one brush with the law as a juvenile in Bakersfield, Linkhauser's record was clean. Married, three kids, owned his trucking firm for ten years; lean times at first, but now his credit rating was solid. The juvenile bust was drug-related, possession of marijuana and driving while impaired, for which he'd gotten probation and loss of his license for six months. Simple kid crime, probably. Unless he was still using and still close to Troy Madison; then it might have some relevance to Madison's bail-jump disappearance. Worth a trip over to Hayward this afternoon to talk to Linkhauser in person. Unless the reason for Coy Madison's call was something more definite.

Yes and no. When Runyon got him on the line, Madison said immediately, "I heard from my brother last night," in a voice that quivered a little. Nervousness, maybe fear.

"Is that right?"

"I know I said I wouldn't let you know if he contacted me, but I thought about it all night and I couldn't just keep quiet, do nothing. Not now."

"He still in the Bay Area?"

"Right here in the city. Hiding out—he wouldn't say where. He wanted money, a lot of money."

"How much is a lot?"

"Ten thousand dollars."

"What did you tell him?"

"That I'd have to talk to Arletta. He gave me an hour, that's all. An hour to try to convince her."

"And did you?"

"No," Madison said. "I didn't talk to her at all."

"Why not?"

"No point in it. She's tightfisted and she already said she wouldn't waste another penny on Troy. She meant it, too. No way she'd let him have ten thousand dollars." Anger and bitterness mixed with the fear now. "I guess I can't blame her, but she doesn't know him the way I do. How dangerous he is when he doesn't get what he wants."

"He threaten you again when you told him he couldn't have the money?"

"Yes. I tried to stall him, reason with him . . . no use. He wouldn't listen. My God, he was furious. He said he'd get Arletta for turning him down. Kill me, too, unless I made her change her mind. He . . . he sounded strung out, crazy."

"You have any idea where he's hiding?"

"No, none. I don't know what to do. I guess that's why I called you—advice. What should I do?"

"Have you contacted the police?"

"No. Not yet."

"You should. Your brother's a fugitive; he's made threats. They can give you protection."

"Yes, but will they? Before it's too late?"

Runyon had no answer for that. A bail-jumping drug dealer was small-time, and the verbal threat of bodily harm had no teeth to it as far as the law was concerned. The detectives at the Hall of Justice had bigger and more immediate crimes to deal with. They'd take Coy Madison's statement; they'd send out patrols to keep an eye on his home and place of business; they'd add to the warrant that was already out on his brother. And that was all they'd do because it was all they could do. No point in saying this to Madison; he probably already knew it. Still, the smart thing in a case like this was to go through the motions—always, no exceptions.

"Call them anyway, Mr. Madison. The sooner the better."

"Isn't there anything else I can do or you can do?"

"One thing, yes. If your brother calls again, tell him your wife has changed her mind and he can have the ten thousand after all. Set up a meeting so you can give him the money."

". . . And then tell you where so you can be there to grab him? Is that the idea?"

"Me or the police."

"Yes, all right. I should've done that when he called last night, shouldn't I? But I wasn't thinking straight." Madison made a deep-breathing sound. "But I doubt he'll call again. As crazy as he sounded last night . . . I'm afraid, Mr. Runyon. For Arletta more than myself."

Runyon asked, "As far as you know, does Troy own a firearm?"

"I don't know. He may have one—he used to go target shooting with a friend of his when we were kids."

"Do you own one?"

"No. Arletta won't have a gun in the house. I could buy one, I suppose. . . ."

"Are you firearms qualified?"

"If you mean have I ever fired a gun . . . no, never. I never liked them."

"Then don't buy one."

"Then how can I protect my wife and myself?"

"Notify the police, first thing. Stay home as much as you can, doors and windows locked. Keep a weapon handy, but not a gun."

"That's all, for God's sake?"

"All that makes good sense, until your brother's caught."

Madison said, "If he's caught, if he doesn't kill Arletta and me first," and broke the connection.

.   .   .

Linkhauser Trucking was a small outfit shoehorned between a couple of larger businesses in an industrial area of Hayward. And none too prosperous, judging from the age of the trucks bearing the company name and the run-down condition of the warehouse building and its two loading bays. Hanging on, like so many small companies in the current economy.

Bud Linkhauser had returned from his Central Valley run; Runyon had made sure he was on schedule before driving down the Peninsula and taking the Santa Mateo Bridge across the bay. Runyon found him on the loading dock, talking to one of his handful of employees. The two of them went inside the warehouse, into a corner where a forklift stood guard over a stack of empty pallets, to do their talking.

You tend to think of truckers as big, beefy guys with potbellies and a gruff manner. Linkhauser didn't fit the stereotype in any of those ways. Short, wiry, losing his hair and compensating for it with a mustache of the same brushy sort Runyon had worn until recently. Soft-spoken and cooperative.

"Nothing much I can tell you," Linkhauser said. "I haven't seen Troy in . . . must be three years now."

"Have you been in touch with his brother or sister-in-law recently?"

"No."

"So you didn't know Troy had been arrested again."

"Not until you told me. Damn shame."

"But you did know he's an addict."

"Meth user, yeah, that's why I had to fire him," Linkhauser said. "He showed up stoned a couple of times, didn't show at all a few others. Unreliable. I got to have men on the job I can count on."

"And you knew he was selling drugs?"

"Well . . . I heard that's how he was supporting himself."

"How'd you hear?"

"From Coy. He tried to get me to give Troy another chance to straighten himself out. I was willing, but the first day he was supposed to come back to work he never showed. After that, well, I just wrote him off. Damn shame, like I said. But what else could I do? I got a business to run and times are tough enough as it is."

"When was that?"

"Three years ago. Last time I saw him."

Runyon said, "I understand you and the Madisons grew up together."

"Down in Bakersfield, right."

"Close friends?"

"I wouldn't say close," Linkhauser said. "Hung out together sometimes."

"Were the brothers close?"

"Not so's you'd notice. Always arguing about something. Coy used to beat up on Troy sometimes."

"Coy did? Not the other way around?"

"Nah. Thing about Troy, he's a mild guy, you know? Shy, laid-back. Go out of his way to avoid a fight."

"And his brother was the opposite?"

"Well, not exactly opposite. Coy's okay until something gets him riled up. Got a temper. Piss him off some way, he'd go after you. That's the way he was as a kid, anyhow."

"Troy have a short fuse, too?"

"No. Real easygoing kid."

"Never retaliated when Coy beat on him?"

"Not that I ever saw."

"Was Troy afraid of Coy?"

"Seemed that way to me."

Runyon said, "Coy must care about his brother, if he tried to get you to help him straighten out."

"Wasn't his idea. It was Troy's."

"Is that right? Then why was Coy the one who contacted you?"

"Troy asked him to," Linkhauser said. "Too shy and ashamed to come to me himself. This was after one of the times he got busted for possession and I guess he figured it was time to get clean. But he was hooked too deep and it didn't last. Went right back on the stuff."

"Would Coy help him on his own, do you think? If he's in big trouble like he is now?"

"Sure, probably." Linkhauser frowned. "Help him run away, you mean?"

"Or hide out."

"I can't answer that, man. It's been three years since I seen either of them, like I said. Who knows what people will do when push comes to shove?"

"Suppose, for the sake of argument, that Coy did want to hide him out. Any place you know of where he might do that?"

Linkhauser shook his head.

Runyon said, "Do you know Jennifer Piper?"

"Who? Oh, that chick Troy was living with. What he saw in a skank like her I'll never understand."

"You know anything about her? Where she comes from, who her friends are?"

"Uh-uh. I only met her once and Troy never talked about her."

"Know any of his friends?"

168 • Bill Pronzini

"No. I never saw him with anybody except the skank."
Linkhauser paused, frowning again. "What'll happen to Troy if
you find him? I mean, how much time in prison will he do?"

"Depends. Three or four years, maximum, if he's convicted
on the dealing charge."

"Better that than being a fugitive, getting himself in deeper
trouble."

"Much better."

Linkhauser looked off toward the loading dock. Thinking
about something, making up his mind. "If Coy is helping
him . . . what happens to him?"

"Harboring a fugitive is a felony," Runyon said. "But it
doesn't have to come to that."

"You wouldn't bring charges against him? Coy?"

"Troy's the man I'm after, not his brother. The quicker I
find him, the better for everybody concerned."

". . . Yeah. Okay, then. Maybe I ought to keep my mouth
shut, but . . . Coy and his wife own a piece of rental property.
Or did, anyway—I think she might've inherited it. They let
Troy stay there for a few weeks after he first moved up from
Bakersfield, until he got a place of his own."

"Where's this property located?"

"Can't tell you that. Might've been S.F., but I'm not sure.
Troy mentioned it once, that's how I know about it, but I
didn't pay much attention to where it was. For all I know, they
could've sold it by now."

"You did the right thing by telling me about it."

"I hope so," Linkhauser said. "It's hard to know what's
best for other people, you know? Half the time I don't even
know what's best for me and my family."

16

Everett Belasco was doing some repair work on his front stoop: down on one knee, a trowel in his right hand and a tray of wet cement beside him. As soon as he saw Helen Alvarez and me coming up his front walk, he put the trowel down and got slowly to his feet.

He looked at me, at Mrs. Alvarez, back at me. "Back again so soon? How come?"

"I've been out talking to Charley Doyle," I said.

"Doyle? Why?"

"I caught him in a lie. About Mrs. Abbott's alleged ghost."

"You mean what happened last night? You don't think Charley—?"

"No, he wasn't the man in the sheet. But he knew of her fancy about her dead husband's ghost when I questioned him two days ago. She only had the notion Monday night, and he hadn't talked to her since he fixed her broken window. Somebody else had to tell him about it."

"Who? Helen?"

"No, not me," she said. I hadn't told her why we were going to see Belasco—I wanted her along as a witness—but she was smart, a lot smarter than Doyle. Or Belasco, for that matter.

From the hostile look she was directing at him, she'd already put two and two together. "I wouldn't give that idiot the time of day."

I said, "Only one other person besides Mrs. Alvarez and me knew. You, Belasco. She mentioned it when we saw you in your garden Tuesday afternoon."

"Me? What about Leonard?"

"I didn't tell him until this morning," Mrs. Alvarez said, "after that sheet nonsense. Or anyone else. Only you."

"And you think I told Charley Doyle? Why would I? I haven't seen or talked to him in weeks."

I said, "When I got here this morning, you were on Mrs. Abbott's porch. Did you go inside the house?"

The sudden shift in questions bewildered Belasco. "Why do you want to know that?"

"Just answer the question. Were you inside her house this morning?"

Mrs. Alvarez answered it for him. "No, he wasn't. Not while I was here."

"Wasn't any reason for me to go in," he said.

"The last time you were in there was when?"

"I don't remember exactly."

"More than a few days?"

"A lot longer than that."

"Do you own a cat?"

"A cat?" Now I really had him off balance. "What's a cat got to do with anything?"

"Oh, quite a bit. You don't own one, do you?"

"No. I don't like cats."

"Are you left-handed, Mr. Belasco?"

". . . What?"

"You heard me. Left-handed."

"No. Right-handed. What the hell—?"

"That bandage on your right hand. This morning you said you cut yourself slicing bacon."

"That's right. So what?"

"When you're doing something like that and the knife slips, the cut is almost always on the *other* hand, the one you're holding the bacon with. Since when does a right-handed man slice a slab of bacon with the knife in his left hand?"

Belasco was sweating now, in spite of the cold. "So maybe I'm ambidextrous. What're you trying to imply?"

"I'm not implying anything. I'm saying that what's under that bandage isn't a knife cut; it's a bite." I held out my hand, palm down, so he had a clear look at the shallow iodine-daubed punctures on the webbing between thumb and forefinger. "A cat bite, just like this one."

"No, no, you're wrong—"

"Take off the bandage and prove it to us."

"No!"

"Doesn't matter, I don't need to see it to know it's a fresh bite, not more than twelve hours old. From the same cat that bit me—Mrs. Abbott's Spike."

Belasco shook his head mutely.

"Spike is an indoor cat, never allowed outside. And he likes to nip strangers when they aren't expecting it. Somebody comes into his house in the middle of the night, he goes to investigate; and if the somebody doesn't like cats, he senses it and does more than just nip the intruder's hand—he gives it a good chomp. Mrs. Abbott was woken up by Spike yowling and she thought it was because the intruder stepped on him. But the real reason he yowled so loud was you swatting or kicking him after he bit you."

"A poor defenseless animal," Mrs. Alvarez said. "You ought to be kicked yourself, Ev Belasco, in a place that'll do the most damage."

He ignored her. "Even if I was bitten by a cat, you can't prove it was Spike. A neighborhood stray—"

"Spike," I said, "and the police lab *can* prove it. Test the bites on my hand and yours, match them to Spike's teeth and saliva. Cat DNA doesn't lie any more than human DNA does."

Belasco shook his head again, but not in denial. He knew he was caught; he'd have to be an idiot like Charley Doyle not to know it.

"You're not only the man in the sheet last night," I said. "You're the one who's been harassing Mrs. Abbott all along. You live right here next door. Easiest thing in the world for you to slip over onto her property in the middle of the night. Hardly any risk at all."

Belasco said, "What reason would I have for hassling an old lady like Margaret?"

"The obvious one—money. A cut of the proceeds from the sale of her property after she was dead or declared incompetent."

"That don't make sense. I'm not a relative of hers—"

"No, but Doyle is," I said. "And you and Charley are buddies, play poker together regularly, have a few private drinks together. He's not very bright and just as greedy as you are. Your brainchild, wasn't it, Belasco? Inspired by that auction fiasco. 'Hey, Charley, why wait until your aunt dies of natural causes—that might take years. Suppose we give her a heart attack, or drive her into an institution . . . either way you get immediate control of her property, then sell it to the Pattersons or some other real estate speculator for a nice fat profit. And I earn my cut by doing all the dirty work while you work up alibis to keep yourself in the clear.' "

"Bastard!" Mrs. Alvarez said fiercely. "Dirty swine!"

A trapped look had come into Belasco's eyes. He stood poised and rigid now, massaging his bandaged hand with the other, as if he were thinking of breaking into a blind run. I hoped he would; I wouldn't have minded popping him for Margaret Abbott's sake.

But he didn't do it. After a few seconds he went all loose and saggy, as if somebody had cut his strings. He took a stumbling step backward, tripped over the lowest of the stairs, and sat down jarringly on the next one above. Then he put his head in his hands.

"I never done anything wrong before in my life," he said. "Never. But the bills been piling up, it's so goddamn hard to live these days, and they been talking about laying people off where I work and I was afraid I'd lose my house . . . ah, God, I don't know. I don't know."

Derisive snort from Helen Alvarez. Nothing from me. I'd heard that kind of self-pitying, self-justifying explanation for criminal behavior too many times before.

Belasco lifted his head, aimed a moist, beseeching look at my client. "I never meant for Margaret to die, Helen. You got to believe that. Just force her out of there so Charley could take over the house, that's all. I like her, she's been a good neighbor. I never meant to hurt her."

Mrs. Alvarez wasn't buying any of that. She called him a couple more names, one of which surprised me and made him cringe. He hid his face in his hands again.

Another small mind at work. Half-wits and knaves, fools and assholes—more of each than ever before, proliferating like weeds in what had started out as a pristine garden. It's a hell of a world we live in, I thought. A hell of a mess we're making of the garden.

Helen Alvarez and I left Belasco sitting there on his stoop— he wasn't going anywhere; he had no place to go and he knew it—and went in to gently break the news to Margaret Abbott. I thought it might be a difficult job, that she'd be shocked and upset hearing that her nephew and a longtime neighbor had both betrayed her trust, but she took it better than I'd expected. I guess maybe you get philosophical about most things, even the evils in the world, when you're eighty-five. Mrs. Alvarez had been and still was considerably more outraged than Mrs. Abbott.

While we were talking, Spike came into the room and hopped up on Mrs. Abbott's lap. She said, stroking him, "You're a hero, dear. Yes, you are." Then she sighed and asked me, "Will both Charley and Everett go to prison?"

"If you press charges against them, they'll probably get some jail time."

"For how long?"

"Breaking and entering, trespassing, malicious destruction of property, intent to defraud, intent to inflict bodily harm . . . with a strict judge, they could each get three years or more."

"Oh. That seems like a long time."

"Not long enough, if you ask me," Helen Alvarez said. "Not *nearly* long enough."

"Do I have to press charges against them?"

The question surprised Mrs. Alvarez. She said, "Of course

you do, Margaret. After what they put you through? How could you *not* press charges?"

"I don't know. Three years behind bars . . ."

"Margaret, listen to me; you can't just let them walk away from this. What if they try something like it again? They could, you know. They're just stupid and venal enough, both of them."

"I suppose you're right. But still . . ."

My cell phone, with its burbling ringtone, interrupted the discussion. Inconvenient as usual, but at least this time I wasn't in the car driving.

Tamara. "I've got that name you asked for this morning. Z.U. at Whitney Middle School."

"Hold on a minute." I excused myself, went out onto the front porch. "Okay, go ahead."

"Zachary Ullman. He's the only Z.U. at the school."

"What's his record like?"

"Clean," she said. "Never been in trouble. Not even so much as a parking ticket."

"Parking ticket? A middle school student can't be old enough to drive."

"He's not a student. Is that what you thought?"

"What is he, then?"

"He's a teacher," Tamara said. "History and social studies. Been at Whitney eleven years."

My God. The tin box, the cocaine . . . one of Emily's *teachers!*

17

TAMARA

Third time roaming around the Western Addition was the charm.

One light brown five-year-old Buick LeSabre parked on Steiner Street a block and a half from Psychic Readings by Alisha.

She'd left work early, headed over to the neighborhood again—compulsive about it now—and her figuring had finally paid off. Fresh excitement made her thump the steering wheel with her fist. She hunted up a parking space for the Toyota, hurried back to the Buick. The right front fender hadn't been visible when she drove by, but she knew it would be scraped and dinged, and it was. No question this was Lucas's car.

She looked both ways along the street. A few pedestrians, but no familiar black face. First thing, she noted the license plate number and quickly wrote it down. Then, casually, as if she owned the damn thing, she tried the passenger side door. Locked. She bent to peer through the window. Front seat: empty. Backseat: empty except for a light jacket that she didn't recognize. Another check of the passersby, and around to the driver's door. Also locked. So no chance at whatever ID items, such as an insurance card, he might keep in the dash compartment.

Not that it mattered, necessarily. The plate number would be enough to ID the registered owner—either Lucas or Mama. Unless they'd switched license plates for some reason . . .

Better not be another dead end, Tamara thought. Not when she was so close . . . better not be.

It wasn't.

The Buick's owner was Alisha J. Delman, with an address in Oxnard. So that was where Mama and Lucas had come from, Southern California. Where they'd been living when the car was registered five years ago, anyhow.

Tamara text-messaged Felice at the SFPD to ask for a quick callback. When Felice complied a few minutes later, she grumbled—as Marjorie at the DMV had grumbled—about being called on too often lately. Some smooth-talking and the promise of a few extra dollars for services rendered and Felice gave in and agreed to run Alisha J. Delman's name through the system.

"Do it ASAP, okay? If you find anything, call me right away. And if there's a mug shot in the file, e-mail it to me."

"Hey, I can't do that," Felice said. "Information is one thing, but I can't be e-mailing files—"

"Oh, hell, Felice. Nobody's looking over your shoulder down there."

"Not right now, maybe. But there's a review coming up next month."

"You worried about that?"

"No, not really, but—"

"Just this one time. I won't ask again."

"Yeah, sure, I've heard that before. Why do you want a mug shot? You're not planning to download it, show it to any-body?"

"No. Just for my own information. I'll delete it right away."

". . . All right, I'll do it for another fifty."

"Damn, girl! You getting greedy now?"

"I need the money, Tam."

"I'll give you twenty-five."

"Uh-uh. Got to be fifty for something like this."

Everybody had their hand out these days, not that you could blame them with the economy in the tank. The fifty dollars would have to come out of her pocket, too.

"Okay, fifty. But this one time only."

"Same with e-mailing files," Felice said.

She called back twenty minutes later. And the info she had was worth five times fifty dollars.

Alisha J. Delman, fifty-three years old, African American, had a record dating back to the mid-1980s. Misdemeanors, mostly, in the L.A. and San Diego areas: operating illegal fortune-telling businesses and offering psychic-reading serv-ices without a license. But there were two felony charges, one for a bait-and-switch con game, the other for a charity swindle that sounded like it might be the prototype of Operation Save—bilking investors in a nonexistent company that was supposed to help black home owners avoid foreclosure. She'd served two years in Tehachapi for her part in the swindle.

But that wasn't the best part.

The best part was that Alisha J. Delman's partner in the charity con was her son from an early marriage, Antoine Del-man, who also had a record—petty theft, impersonating a police officer for purposes of fraud, bunco schemes like the bait-and-switch con—and who'd also been convicted and also served time in prison for the same swindle.

Antoine. Antoine Delman.

And Mama really was his mama.

Alisha and Antoine, the two A's—A for "Assholes." Everything Tamara had thought they were, and more.

Felice e-mailed a mug shot of him as well as Alisha and that proved it beyond any doubt. He hadn't worn a mustache back then, but there was no mistaking that blocky face and hooked nose and receding hairline. Mama surprised Tamara a little. From that scratchy old voice on the phone she'd expected a witchlike crone, but Alisha was just the opposite—slim and attractive, with the big soulful eyes of a black madonna. No wonder she'd been able to run her psychic scams so easily.

Decision time again.

If Antoine and Alisha had been wanted for anything, what to do now would've been an easy choice: call the law and turn them in. But they'd served their sentences and they weren't fugitives. And as far as Tamara knew or could prove, they hadn't actually done anything in the Bay Area yet except five-finger the real Lucas Zeller's briefcase, a theft that couldn't be proved beyond a reasonable doubt, and set up their marks for a new version of the black charity con. Money had to change hands, a large sum of it, in front of witnesses in order for a felony fraud charge to stick.

She could still go to the police, but it wouldn't be easy convincing them to act. All she had was conjecture—no evidence or corroborative witnesses. Bringing Deron Stewart in wouldn't do any good; all he knew was what she'd told him, what she'd hired him to do. The fraud inspectors would want to know who she was representing, the details of her investigation, where she'd gotten the data on the Delmans' criminal histories. No way would she compromise Felice, and the truth about why she was after the Delmans would make her actions look like a personal vendetta (which it damn well was) and might even leave her open to charges of misuse of her license for acting as her own unpaid client.

The only way to get quick action was with evidence that kept the cops' focus off of her and on Antoine and Mama and their con game. That meant finding out more about how they'd set it up, how much money they'd scored so far, and when they were expecting the rest to be paid. It also meant convincing at least one of the victims that they were being conned, then convincing them to take a trip to the Hall of Justice.

Four options there. No, make that three. Wait and do nothing until after the down-low club's meeting on Saturday night was out. Deron Stewart might be able to get her some of what she needed and he might not; he might even screw up and blow the whole deal. If the two A's got even a whiff that their scam had been found out, they'd take off like a shot.

Okay, three options—the three people she knew for sure were marks. Doctor Easy, Viveca Inman, Judge Alfred Mantle. Which one had the most knowledge? Which one was the most vulnerable?

Doctor Easy? No. She just wasn't sure enough of where he stood. A man with a past record like his was as untrustworthy as they made 'em.

Inman? No. She knew Mama, she knew about Operation Save, but she might be hard to convince if Alisha had her hooks in deep enough. People into psychics the way Viveca

Inman was would fight like hell to keep from admitting they'd put their faith in crooks.

That left Judge Mantle. She thought about him a little, and . . . oh yeah, he was the best choice. The perfect choice, matter of fact—just so long as she stayed cool and handled him the right way, no mistakes.

18

Zachary David Ullman lived in Daly City, in one of the houses that march in long, close ranks up and down across the spines of the hills overlooking Candlestick Park, the bay, SFO. Ticky-tacky houses, Malvina Reynolds called them in her sixties song "Little Boxes." Ullman's was exactly like all the others on his street except for its color, dark brown with pale blue trim, and a couple of stunted yew trees along the front wall next to the garage.

It was after five when I pulled up in front. Fog rolled sinuously along the winding street, up and around the houses, blotting out the bay view. Three hundred days a year it would be either foggy or windy up here; the people who bought these homes on one of the few clear days and expected to enjoy regular sunny vistas would always be disappointed.

I sat in the car for a couple of minutes, looking over at Ullman's house. A not very new Hyundai sat on the cracked concrete driveway and there was a light on behind a curtained front window above the garage, so he was home. He apparently lived alone; the only blot, if you could call it that, on his exemplary record was a divorce nine years ago. He was thirty-five, had no children of his own.

Anger had ridden with me on the drives to the condo to pick up the tin box and then on up here, but I had it tamped down now. Mostly. I wanted to be sure I was in complete control before I went over there and had my talk with Ullman. Getting in his face, hurling accusations, figured to be counterproductive. The situation called for a more subtle approach. I had no real proof that the tin box belonged to him; the fact that he was the only Z.U. at Whitney Middle School was circumstantial at best. You had to be very careful in a case like this, where a man's livelihood and reputation were at stake. The last thing I could afford was a lawsuit.

Still, I had a feeling he was the right Z.U. Emily always responded to authority figures; I should have remembered that. She was more likely to believe and let herself be talked into protecting a teacher than one of her classmates. It wasn't the probable fact that Ullman was a recreational coke user that had me so upset; it was the way he'd used and manipulated Emily. That and bringing cocaine onto school grounds, as he must have done, and then being careless enough to lose the box there. Where else would she have found it?

Okay. I got out and crossed the street, hunching against the bite of the wind-driven fog. The entrance to Ullman's house was on the side away from the garage, up a short, inclined path and a short flight of concrete steps. A few seconds after I rang the bell, a dead-bolt lock clicked and the door swung inward.

He was slightly built, with regular features and thinning caramel-colored hair, wearing slacks and a tan sweater with suede elbow patches. He did a mild double take when he saw me, his eyes widening and blinking—soft brown eyes, like a melancholy hound's, eyes that could melt the heart of a naïve thirteen-year-old girl. Expecting someone else, I thought, and caught off balance to see a stranger standing here instead. None too pleased about it. And suddenly nervous.

"Yes? May I help you?"

"Zachary Ullman?"

"Yes? If you're selling something—"

"I'm not." I told him my name, nothing more. It didn't seem to mean anything to him. "My daughter is a student at Whitney Middle School."

"Is she? In one of my classes?"

"That's right. Her name is Emily."

It took him about three seconds to put that together with my last name. His expression didn't change, but his body language did; you could see him drawing up tight, so tight that his posture straightened into a stiff vertical line. He made an effort to keep his voice even and polite when he said, "Yes, of course—Emily," but it didn't quite come off.

"Mind if we talk inside? Pretty cold out here."

"I . . . no, I'm sorry." He moved forward half a step, widening his stance, as if he were afraid I might try to push my way inside. "I really don't have the time right now. If you'd like to make an appointment for a consultation at the school—"

"Now, Mr. Ullman. It won't wait."

"What won't wait? Why are you here?"

I took the tin box out of my pocket, held it up in the palm of my hand. He had to look, but only for a couple of seconds before his gaze shifted. He was holding on to the edge of the door and I saw his fingers clench, the tendons in his wrist stand out like cords. The pressure made the door move slightly from side to side.

He said, "Is that supposed to mean something to me?"

186 • Bill Pronzini

"Yours, isn't it?"

"It is not. Did Emily tell you it belongs to me?"

"Emily didn't tell me anything."

"Then what makes you think it's mine?"

"It has your initials on it."

"*My* initials?"

"Z.U."

"Yes, well? They're uncommon, but I'm sure quite a few other people have them."

"Not at Whitney Middle School."

". . . Just why are you here?"

"I think you know."

"I don't know. How did you find out where I live?"

I just looked at him.

"I tell you, that box isn't mine," Ullman said. "I've never seen it before. Anyone could have scratched my initials on it."

"On purpose, to implicate you?"

"Implicate me in what? What are you implying?"

"Not implying, stating. I think the box is yours."

"I've just told you—"

"The box, and what was inside it."

"I have no idea what you're talking about."

The hell he didn't. He was so twitchy inside that rigid body you could almost see him vibrating, like sensitive machinery whirring away within a pliant casing. The door kept wobbling, as if he were struggling against the urge to slam it shut in my face.

The sound of an approaching car grew out of the fog behind me. Ullman heard it and his gaze slid away from mine again, past me to the street. Headlights crawled through the wet mist, brightening as the car drew abreast of the house.

When it went on past without slowing, he tongued his upper lip, his Adam's apple working, and then looked at me again.

"Cocaine," I said.

". . . What?"

"Inside the box. A little tube of cocaine."

He said, "What?" again, trying to sound surprised; that didn't come off, either.

"Emily found it at your school," I said.

"Then it must belong to one of her classmates. I'm a *teacher,* for heaven's sake—"

"Teachers have been known to use cocaine recreationally. But the smart ones use it in the privacy of their own homes. They don't bring it to school and then lose it where kids can stumble on it."

". . . Did she tell you she found it at Whitney?"

"Didn't I just say she hasn't told me anything? She honors her promises, particularly those she makes to adults."

"I have no idea what you mean."

I could feel my blood pressure rising. "Deny and stonewall, right, Ullman? If Emily does admit what she knows and what you made her promise, it's her word against yours—a kid's word against an adult's."

". . . What do you intend to do?"

"What would you do if you were me?"

"I'd be very careful of my facts before I accused someone of using illegal drugs. Very, very careful. Otherwise . . ."

"Otherwise what?"

"I'm not a litigious man," he said, "but if you try to sully my name and my reputation with the school board, I'll sue for slander and defamation. I mean that; I—"

Another car appeared on the street, this one going faster

than the last one. Ullman's gaze went to it, magnetically. Stayed fixed on it until it passed on by and out of sight.

He was really vibrating now. The brown hound's eyes showed an odd mix of emotions—melancholy, anger, fear. Hunted eyes, I thought, haunted eyes.

"What's got you so upset, Ullman?"

"What do you think? You coming here, making accusations . . ."

"Is that all?"

"Isn't it enough? You have no right—"

I said, "I wonder if there are fingerprints."

". . . What?"

"On the box. Or on the tube." There wouldn't be—the surfaces were too rough on one, too smooth on the other, and they'd both been handled too much anyway for clear latents— but I wanted to see what he'd say.

"That's . . . ridiculous," he said. "What do you know about fingerprints?"

"Quite a bit. It's my business to know about things like that."

"Your business? I don't . . . Who are you?" The obvious answer smacked him and made him jerk, turned him a little white around the gills. "You . . . you're not a policeman?"

"I was once. Now I'm a private investigator. And I still have contacts in law enforcement."

"A private—" He shook his head a couple of times, hard, the way you do after you've just come up out of a particularly frightening nightmare and you're not quite sure yet it wasn't real. "I have nothing more to say to you. Just . . . leave me alone. You understand? Leave me alone!"

This time he went ahead and slammed the door in my face.

I moved down to the sidewalk and on to my car, taking my time in spite of the night's chill. The one time I glanced up, I spotted a gap at one corner of the curtained front window, Ullman's face framed there: watching to make sure I left or looking for whoever he was expecting, or maybe both.

My car was parked some distance upstreet and he couldn't have had a clear look at it through the churning mist. My advantage. I didn't waste any time getting in and driving away, but I only went a couple of blocks, around a long curve to where I couldn't be seen from Ullman's place. Then I made a U-turn and parked and sat in the darkened car with the engine running. After three minutes by the dashboard clock, I rolled back around the curve, slow, with the driver's window down and my lights off — not too smart on a foggy night, but the street remained deserted. Fifty yards or so from Ullman's house, I had a misty view of the front entrance and the lighted front window. He wasn't looking out now; the curtain was drawn tight at both corners.

There was room to park at the curb on my side. I drifted over, killed the engine. And sat there waiting.

Trust your hunches. The one I had about Zachary Ullman was strong enough to warrant some more of my time. His edginess was only partly due to my unexpected arrival and the conversation we'd had. He hadn't wanted me inside the house, for one thing. And he hadn't wanted me there when his visitor or visitors showed up. Why? The only reason I could think of was that he had something to hide, something he didn't want a stranger and especially a detective to know about.

Time passed. Crept, rather, the way it always does on any kind of stakeout. Passive waiting has never been my long suit.

As far as I'm concerned, Ambrose Bierce had it right in his *Devil's Dictionary* definition of patience: a minor form of despair disguised as a virtue.

I kept shifting around on the seat, huddled inside my coat, because of incipient leg cramps and because my lower back was giving me trouble again. Getting too old for this kind of thing, sitting alone in cars on cold nights. I was supposed to be semiretired, wasn't I? At home in the evenings, in the warm condo with my family?

Sure, but this was something that threatened a family member and by extension threatened me. And made me suspicious as well as angry. I didn't like that son of a bitch in the house across the street; at the very least he was a liar and a cokehead. I'd sit here, never mind the cramps and lower back pain, for as long as it took to see if my hunch panned out.

Not long, fortunately. Not much more than fifteen minutes.

Headights appeared around the curve behind me, the fourth set I'd seen since I'd been here, but this vehicle was going more slowly than the others; and as soon as it passed me, it coasted over to the curb just up ahead. Old, beat-up van, light and dark two-tone in color.

The lights flicked off, and a stick of a man wearing a sleeveless down jacket got out and came around to open one of the rear doors, take something out. Two somethings—a two-foot-long cardboard mailing tube, looked like, and a package about the size of a shoe box. I'd been thinking Ullman was waiting for the Man, but cocaine doesn't get transported in mailing tubes, or in shoe boxes unless the buyer is stocking up by the kilo.

I watched the stick figure cross the street with his two

parcels. In the foggy darkness I couldn't tell much about him except that he seemed middle-aged and had stringy shoulder-length hair that the wind whipped around his head. Nothing furtive about him—just a guy on his way to somebody's house, invited guest or deliveryman.

Ullman opened up right away, as he had with me. Let the long-haired man inside, poked his head back out to look up and down the street—if he noticed my car, it didn't hold his attention—and then quickly shut the door.

For a minute or so I kept my eyes on the window curtain. Neither corner moved. I reached up and unscrewed the dome light, waited another minute, and when Ullman's door stayed shut I got out and walked up close enough to the van to read the license plate. Personalized: *DDTDAWG*. Easy to remember, even with a porous memory like mine.

Back in the car, I rolled the window all the way up; I'd done enough freezing for tonight. I thought about following DDT-DAWG when he left, but why bother? The license number was enough for me to find out who he was. But I waited anyway, out of curiosity as to how long he'd stay with Ullman.

Too long to be an average deliveryman, not long enough to be an invited guest. A little less than ten minutes. The door opened, out DDTDAWG came, the door closed. He climbed into his van without a glance in my direction, drove away into the fog.

Two minutes later, when the light in Ullman's front window went out, I took myself out of there, too, with the heater going full blast. I was almost warm by the time I got home.

19

JAKE RUNYON

It was only four thirty when Runyon left Bud Linkhauser and walked out of the trucking company warehouse, but when he called the agency he got the answering machine. Either Tamara was with a client or she'd closed up early for some reason. He put on the Bluetooth device he'd bought when the no-hands cell phone law went into effect, tried again as he was dead-stopped in commute traffic on the San Mateo Bridge approach. Machine again. She must have gone for the day.

He called her cell number. Voice mail. Then he tried her home number. Answering machine.

So he'd have to run a property search himself when he got back to the city. He'd done it before. Easy work if you knew which city and county the property was in, harder when you didn't, but if Coy and Arletta still owned the rental, it shouldn't take him too long to find out.

Wrong.

In his cold apartment on Ortega, he booted up his laptop and went through the property records for San Francisco first; then, when that didn't turn up anything in either Coy or

Arletta Madison's name, he searched the rest of the Bay Area counties one by one. No listing.

Linkhauser had said the property might've been inherited by Arletta Madison. Since she controlled the family purse strings, it was possible she'd kept it on the tax rolls under her maiden name. Runyon checked his files. Maiden name: Hoffman. He repeated the county-by-county search. No listing.

Two possibilities, then. The rental property had been sold. Or one or both Madisons still owned it, but the ownership was listed under a different name, such as a family trust. Tamara could find out either way, but he didn't have her computer skills or search engine knowledge.

He tried her cell number again; she still wasn't answering. She wasn't home, either: her machine again.

Wait until tomorrow? That would mean sitting around the empty apartment all evening with the TV on for noise. Bryn had an art class tonight, wouldn't be home until late. Better to be out and moving. The Madisons might not be willing to talk to him about the rental property, but there was no harm in trying. At least he'd be able to judge by their reactions, Coy's in particular, whether or not that was where Troy Madison and his girlfriend were hiding out.

There were lights on in the Queen Anne Victorian, but nobody answered the bell. Could be one or both of the Madisons were holed up inside, but if that was the case, why leave all the lights on? And why not check to see who was waiting out here? There was a peephole in the door, but Runyon didn't hear any footsteps on the hardwood floor inside.

He'd parked his Ford a short way up the block; he went and sat behind the wheel without moving. Might as well wait awhile. People don't usually leave so many lights blazing when they went out for an entire evening.

Cars came up and down the street now and then, but none of them parked in the vicinity. It was after eight now and there weren't any pedestrians. Foggy shadows obscured most of the paths and lawns on this edge of Dolores Park.

He hadn't been there long when he saw the woman.

She was on the far side of 19th Street, coming uphill alongside the park. Alone, bundled in a coat and some kind of cloth cap, walking briskly. He watched her progress because she appeared to be the size and shape of Arletta Madison. If that's who she was, she'd cross over once she drew abreast of the Madison Victorian.

She didn't cross the street. Started to, he thought, but she didn't have time.

A line of trees and low shrubs flanked the sidewalk where she was, with a separating strip of lawn about twenty yards wide. The tall figure of a man came out of the tree-shadow as she passed. Runyon couldn't see him clearly through the fog, but he had one arm up in front of him, a familiar black shape jutting from a gloved hand. And he didn't have a face—it was hidden beneath something dark pulled down tight over his head.

Gun. Ski mask.

Runyon reacted instinctively. His .357 Magnum was locked in the glove box; there was no time for him to go after it. He hit the door handle, piled out of the car. The mugger was ten yards from the woman and closing. She'd heard him and was turning toward him; he lunged forward, grabbing at the shoulder-strap purse she carried. Runyon pounded across the street, his shoes slipping on the wet pavement, yelling at the top of his voice, "Hold it; police officer!"—the only words likely to have an effect in a situation like this.

Not this time.

The mugger's head swiveled in Runyon's direction, swiveled back to the woman as she pulled away from him. She made a frightened, chicken-squawking sound and turned to run.

He shot her.

No compunction: just threw the gun up and fired point-blank.

She went down, skidding on her side, as Runyon cut between two parked cars onto the sidewalk. The mugger pumped a round at him then. He was already dodging sideways, onto the lawn, when he saw the muzzle flash, heard the whine of the bullet and the low, flat crack of the weapon. The grass was thick and mist soggy; his feet slid out from under him and he went planing forward on his ass, clawing at the turf and trying to twist his body toward the nearby shrubbery. Out there in the open, with only twenty yards or so separating him from the gun, he made a hell of a target.

But the mugger didn't fire again. Most of them were cowards and when they lost the elements of surprise and control their instincts were to run. By the time Runyon checked his momentum and squirmed around, this one was running splay-footed back into the park. Shadows and fog swallowed him within seconds.

Runyon had banged the knee on his bad leg in the fall; it sent out twinges as he hauled himself erect, hobbled toward the woman. She was still down but not hurt as badly as he'd feared: sitting up on one hip now, holding her left arm cradled in against her breast. The woolen cap had been knocked askew when she went down; the wind whipped long, stringy hair around the pale oval of her face. When she heard him coming, she looked up with fright-bugged eyes.

Arletta Madison, all right.

She blinked at him without recognition when he hunkered down beside her. He said, "It's all right, he's gone now."

"He shot me," she said in a dazed voice.

"Where are you hurt?"

"My arm—"

"Shoulder? Forearm?"

"Above the elbow."

"Can you move it?"

"I don't . . . yes, I can move it."

Not too bad then. The bullet hadn't struck bone.

She blinked at him again, with clearer focus. "You're the man who was here yesterday. The detective . . . Runyon."

"Yes." You weren't supposed to move gunshot victims, but her wound didn't seem serious and he couldn't just let her sit here on the wet street. "Can you stand up, walk?"

"If you help me . . ."

He wrapped an arm around her waist, lifted her. The blood was visible then, glistening blackly on the sleeve of her coat.

"My purse," she said.

It was lying on the sidewalk nearby. Runyon let go of her long enough to pick it up. She took it from him with her good hand, clutched it tightly against her chest: something solid and familiar to hang on to.

The street was still empty; so were the sidewalks on both sides and what he could see of the park. Somebody was standing behind a lighted window in one of the duplexes across 19th, peering through parted drapes. No one else seemed to have heard the shots, or to want to know what had happened if they did. City dwellers didn't come out to investigate gun-shots these days: too many drive-by shootings, too much random violence.

Runyon helped Arletta Madison across the street, walking with his arm around her and her body braced against his as if they were a pair of lovers. Get her off the street and into her house as quickly as possible, to where she'd feel safe, and report the shooting and ask for EMTs from there.

As they started up the front stoop, she drew a shuddering breath and said in a hoarse whisper, "God, he could have killed me," as if the realization had just struck her. "I could be dead right now."

"He say anything before he shot you?"

"Say anything? No. He just . . . shot me." Then, at the door, "Coy was right, damn him."

"Right about what?"

"He keeps telling me not to go out alone at night, and I keep not listening. I'm so goddamn smart, I am. Nothing ever happened; I thought nothing ever would. . . ."

"You learned a lesson," he said. "Don't hurt yourself any more than you already are."

"I hate it when he's right." She opened her purse with her good hand, fumbled inside. "Where the hell did I put the damn keys?"

Runyon found them for her, unlocked the door. Upstairs, she steered him into a big front room full of heavy old furniture and dominated by more of her weird vegetable-like sculptures. She dropped her purse on a brocade couch, let him help her out of her coat. The wound in her arm was still leaking blood; the crimson splotch on the sleeve of a white sweater had grown to the size of a pancake.

"Are you in much pain?"

"No. It's mostly numb."

"Where's the nearest bathroom?"

"Down the hall there."

He walked her to it. "Better get out of that sweater," he said then. "Put some peroxide on the wound, then wrap a wet towel around it. That should do until the EMTs get here."

"Are you going to call the police?"

"Yes."

"They'll never catch whoever it was; you know they won't."

"I have to report the shooting in any case. And you're going to need attention for that arm."

"All right," she said. Then, in different tones, "Actually, I suppose the publicity will be good for me and my next show."

He made the call while she was in the bathroom. The 911 dispatcher asked the usual questions, said that EMTs and police would be out ASAP. Which meant half an hour, minimum, for the paramedics; their first responses were Code 3 or Echo priority, the situations in which injuries were life threatening or resuscitation was required, and there were plenty of those every night in the city. The cops wouldn't be here in a hurry, either: perp long gone, victim not seriously wounded, situation under control. They'd just have to wait their turn.

Pretty soon Arletta Madison reappeared, wearing a sleeveless blouse now, a towel wrapped around her arm. Runyon asked her if the wound was still bleeding. She said, "Yes, but not so badly now." Then, "*Damn* Coy. This is his fault, you know."

"How so?"

"When he pisses me off the way he did tonight, I get so mad I feel the walls start closing in."

"And then you go out for a walk."

"To cool off, yes."

"What'd he do to upset you tonight?"

"The usual crap. Called from some bar on Twenty-fourth Street, drunk, to tell me he'd just picked up a woman. Can you believe it?"

Runyon said nothing.

"I swear he does it just to devil me. He doesn't give a damn about me; he . . . *oh!* Shit!" She'd made the mistake of trying to gesture with her wounded arm. "Where the hell are the paramedics?"

"They'll be here pretty soon."

"I need a drink. Or don't you think I should have one?"

"I wouldn't. They'll give you something for the pain."

"Well, they'd better hurry. How about you? Do you want something?"

"No."

"Suit yourself. But you don't have to stand there; go ahead and sit down."

"You'd better do the same."

"I'm too restless."

"Sit down, Mrs. Madison. For your own good."

The command made her narrow her eyes at him, but she didn't argue. She sank onto the couch, grimaced, and chewed on her lower lip. Runyon waited until her expression told him the pain had eased before he spoke again.

"I need to ask you some questions, if you feel up to it."

"Questions? About what?"

"A rental property you own or owned."

". . . What the hell does that have to do with anything?"

"It's the reason I came here tonight. I've been told you inherited property in the Bay Area."

"Yes, but I don't see—"

"Do you still own it?"

Head bob. "For all the good it's doing us now."

"Not rented at present?"

"Not since the last tenant's lease expired at the end of December."

"Where's the property located? Here in the city?"

"No. San Bruno."

"Single-family house?"

"Yes. It's not in the best neighborhood, that's why it's still—" She broke off, frowning. "Why are you asking about this? You don't think—"

"Don't think what, Mrs. Madison?"

"That that's where Troy is hiding?"

"Possible, isn't it?"

"I suppose so, if he knows about the property."

"You didn't tell him about it? Give him a key at some point?"

"Of course not. The rental agent has the keys." Her frown morphed into a scowl. "He'd better not be there," she said. "I won't stand for that on top of the money he's cost me. If you think that's where he is, why don't you go find out?"

"You'll have to give me the address."

"It's on Bowerman Street in San Bruno, I don't remember the number. I'll have to look it up."

"After the EMTs get here."

"If they ever get here."

Runyon said, "Your husband tell you about Troy's latest call?"

"Call? When?"

"Last night. Demanding ten thousand dollars. Making threats when he was told he couldn't have it."

"No, Coy never said a word. Threatened us? You mean, with physical harm?"

"So he told me."

"Damn him! And tonight he leaves me here alone—" She broke off and sat very still, not looking at Runyon any longer but at something that had begun playing on the screen of her mind. A kind of slow horror parted her lips, widened her eyes. "Oh my God," she said. "What just happened outside . . . that man in the mask . . . Troy? Could it have been *Troy?*"

Before Runyon could respond, a door banged below. Heavy, plodding footfalls sounded on the stairs. A few seconds later Coy Madison came duck-waddling in from the hall.

20

JAKE RUNYON

Madison stopped abruptly two paces inside the room, stood blinking his surprise at Runyon and then at his wife. He wore an overcoat over a suit and tie, no hat; his red hair was damp, his smooth cheeks and forehead red blotched.

"Good Christ, Arletta," he said, "what happened to you? That towel . . . is that blood?"

"I was attacked a few minutes ago. He shot me."

"*Shot* you? Who . . . ?"

She shook her head.

Madison went and sat next to her, tried to wrap an arm around her shoulders. She pushed him away.

He said, "The wound . . . it's not serious?"

"No. But it hurts like the devil." She grimaced again. "What's *keeping* those paramedics?"

"You get a good look at the man who did it?"

"No. He was wearing a mask."

"A mask? Where'd this happen?"

"Outside by the park. Mr. Runyon chased him off. If he hadn't been there, I'd probably be dead right now."

Madison bounced up and waddled over to Runyon, close enough for Runyon to get a whiff of his breath. "I'm grateful you came when you did," he said. "But why? You haven't found my brother yet?"

"Not yet."

"Then . . ." His thin mouth tightened. "Troy," he said.

Runyon waited.

"Maybe it wasn't a mugger who shot Arletta; maybe it was my brother. He threatened us, I told you that."

"Why didn't you tell *me?*" Arletta Madison said. "Didn't you think I had a right to know?"

"I didn't want to worry you."

"Didn't want to worry me. You bastard, you were so worried you went out and got drunk and tried to get yourself laid."

"I wasn't trying to get laid. I was upset, I wanted a couple of drinks to calm down. I shouldn't have done it, I shouldn't have called you from that bar—I should've come straight home."

"Bloody well right you should."

"All right, I'm sorry. But why didn't you stay in the house instead of going out alone in the dark?"

"Don't start in, Coy. I'm in no mood for it."

Madison waved an agitated hand. "Troy . . . sure. He must've been over there watching the house, waiting for his chance. If you hadn't gone out, he might've broken in. But you made it easy for him. How many times have I warned you it's not safe to go traipsing around this neighborhood at night? You just won't listen."

"I said don't start in. It's as much your fault as mine."

"Oh sure, blame it all on me. Twist everything around so you don't have to take responsibility."

Her arm was hurting her and the pain made her vicious.

She bared her teeth at him. "What're you doing home any-way? Where's the bimbo you claimed you picked up?"

"I brushed her off. I started thinking about you here alone—"

"Sure, right. You were drunk; now you're sober. If there was any brushing off, she's the one who did it."

"Arletta . . ."

"What's the matter with your face? She give you some kind of rash?"

"My face? There's nothing wrong with my face—"

"It looks like a rash. It better not be contagious."

"Goddamn it, Arletta—"

Runyon had had enough of this. The bickering, the hatred, the cold deception—everything about the two of them. He said in a flat, hard voice, "All right, both of you shut up."

They stared at him. Arletta Madison said, "You can't talk to me like that in my own home—"

"Keep your mouth closed and your ears open for five min-utes and you'll learn something. Your husband and I will do the talking."

Madison said, glowering, "I don't have anything more to say to you."

"Yeah, you do. A lot more."

"Why'd you come here tonight anyway? I'm glad you showed up in time to chase Troy off, but if you'd done your job and found him before—"

"I have found him," Runyon said.

"What?"

"I know where he is."

". . . Where?"

"The rental house in San Bruno. Where you hid him out."

"Where *I* hid him? Man, you're crazy."

His wife said, "Coy, what—"

"Shut up," he said without looking at her. He wasn't looking at Runyon, either. His gaze seemed fixed on the hand he kept waving loosely in the air. "If that's where my brother is, he went there on his own. I had nothing to do with it."

"Then why didn't you tell me about the rental property?"

"I don't know; it never occurred to me."

"You didn't want me to know about Bud Linkhauser, either. Afraid he'd tell me enough so I'd figure out you engineered the whole thing."

"I don't know what you're talking about."

"Sure you do. Troy jumping bail wasn't his idea, or the Piper woman's. It was yours. You talked him into it."

"Why would I want him to jump bail, for Chrissake?"

"Same reason you arranged his bail in the first place. To get him out of jail, then make a fugitive out of him."

"Bullshit. What reason would I have to do a crazy thing like that? Didn't I tell you how violent he can be, all the threats he made?"

"You told me a lot of things, most of them lies. The truth is, you're the violent one, not Troy."

Madison was so worked up now he kept shifting from one foot to another, like a kid who needed to go to the toilet. "No! He used to beat me up when we were kids—"

"Not according to Bud Linkhauser. He says you were the aggressor."

"What the hell does Linkhauser know about the way things are now? Maybe I had some control over Troy once, but that all changed when he got into drugs. He *threatened* us, goddamn it! He threatened to kill Arletta and me!"

"So you keep saying, emphasizing. All part of your plan."

"Plan? What plan?"

"To murder your wife and frame your brother for it."

Him: hissing intake of breath.

Her: strangled bleating noise.

"He's the one who shot you tonight, Mrs. Madison. Not a mugger, not Troy—your husband. The only reason you're alive is that he doesn't know enough about firearms to shoot straight in the dark."

Him: "That's a fucking lie!"

Her, to Runyon in a ground-glass voice: "Coy? How can you know it was Coy?"

"You told me he was drunk when he called you earlier. He wasn't, he was faking it. Nobody can sober up that fast in an hour, not when he's standing here now without any smell of alcohol on his breath. The call was designed to do just what it did, drive you out of the house."

Madison took a step forward, changed his mind. He still wouldn't meet Runyon's gaze, or his wife's. He wore the guilty man's look now—sick and self-pitying.

Runyon said, "I had a pretty good look at the shooter as he was running away. Tall—and your husband's tall, but his brother's four inches shorter. Walked and ran splayfooted, like a duck—the way he walks. Then there're those blotches on his face. Look at them close-up and you can see they're not a rash. He's got the kind of skin that takes and holds imprints from fabric, doesn't he? Wakes up in the morning with pillow and blanket marks on his face? The ones he's got now are from the ribbing of that ski mask."

"You son of a bitch!" she said to Madison. "You dirty son of a bitch!"

She came up off the couch and went for him with nails flashing. Runyon got in her way, grabbed hold of her; her injured arm stopped her from struggling with him. Then Madison tried to make a run for it. Runyon let go of her, chased him, and caught him at the head of the stairs. When Madison tried to kick him, Runyon knocked him flat on his skinny ass.

With perfect timing, the doorbell rang. And it wasn't just the EMTs; the law had also arrived.

Coy Madison was as stupid as they come. The weapon he'd used, a Saturday night special, and the ski mask were both in the trunk of his car.

Once he was confronted with the evidence, he broke down and spewed out a confession. It was all pretty much as Runyon had figured it, right down to the motive. Madison hated his wife, was jealous of her success, wanted control of her money and their joint property. No feelings for his brother, either, other than contempt for Troy's drugged-out lifestyle, so the idea had been to get rid of both of them together. Kill her, then drive down to the rental house in San Bruno and plant the gun and ski mask on Troy, then phone in an anonymous tip to the police, and when Troy told them the bail-jump was his brother's idea deny the hell out of it. The word of an allegedly honest citizen against that of an addict, dealer, and fugitive. Which of them would be believed?

Foolproof plan, in Coy's view. Stupid plan, in Runyon's. A rookie cop with a couple of ounces of imagination could have seen through it, even if Madison hadn't screwed it up with lies of commission and omission, a bumbling murder attempt, and a too-quick return home to find out how badly his wife was wounded. He didn't realize yet how lucky he was that he hadn't fired a killing shot. As it was, the charges would be attempted murder and aiding and abetting a fugitive; if he stayed lucky, he might still be relatively young when he got out of prison.

While Madison was confessing, his wife hurled invective at him and the inspectors had to keep warning her to be quiet. She would have cut his throat with a dull knife if they'd let her have one. She told him so, complete with chains of four-letter words.

Runyon was glad when they let him leave. He'd have liked to be the one to pick up Troy Madison and Jennifer Piper and deliver them to the Hall of Justice, but once he'd explained where they were hiding it was out of his hands. Didn't really matter; the fact that he'd been responsible for putting the jumper back in custody would be enough to satisfy Abe Melikian. But Runyon prided himself on being able to close his cases himself, hands on.

At least he'd been the one to blow up Coy Madison's idiot scheme. Satisfaction enough in that, even if it was only a by-product of the job he'd been assigned to do.

21

TAMARA

Judge Alfred Mantle was doing pretty well for himself. His house in Monterey Heights, on one of the winding streets below Mt. Davidson, was one of those big Spanish-style jobs you saw in the city's upper-class residential districts. Lots of fancy tile, lots of shrubbery and tall, thin cypress trees. House lights, porch light, spotlights strewn among the landscaping— all blazing in the foggy early-evening gloom. Not many black folks could afford to live up here; sure bet that most, if not all, of the judge's neighbors were white.

Tamara drove on past, parked a little ways above the house. She didn't really want to be here, but on the phone he'd said she could either come here tonight—his wife wasn't home and wouldn't be back until late—or see him in his chambers at City Hall sometime tomorrow. Pretty obvious why he wouldn't agree to meet her on neutral ground. In his house or in his chambers, he'd have the psychological upper hand. Or thought he would.

The street and sidewalk were wet and the cypress trees dripped, a kind of lonely, desolate sound. But nothing could dampen her spirits tonight, not unless she screwed up with the judge—and she wasn't going to let that happen. All she'd told him on the phone was who she was, that she needed to talk to him about the Operation Save fund and the man he knew as Lucas Zeller, and that it'd be in his best interest to meet with her ASAP. He'd asked a bunch of questions that she'd pretty much evaded; the answers were better given face-to-face. He made it plain that he didn't like being approached this way, by a private investigator of either sex, but in the end he agreed to see her.

She rang the bell, listened to chimes floating around inside. There was one of those one-way magnifying glass peepholes in the door and she had the feeling he was right there on the other side looking out at her, sizing her up in the bright porch light before he let her in.

She did a little sizing up of her own when he finally opened the door. Up close he was even huskier than he'd seemed at a distance. Large head and thick neck, like a football player. Real judge's face: stern eyes, streaks of gray in the curly black of his hair, and an expression blank as a wall.

The first thing he said to her was, "You're not what I expected, Ms. Corbin."

"No? Not a sister, you mean?"

"Not a sister and not so young. You sounded older on the phone."

"I'm not as young as I look," she lied.

He stood aside to let her come in. When he shut the door behind her he said, "We'll talk in my study," and didn't quite put his back to her as they moved through the house.

Some house. The furniture was modern and expensive, the décor black and white, mostly, with lots of African sculptures and carvings and such on shelves and in nooks and crannies. His wife's doing—Tamara knew that as soon as she walked into his study. Everything in there—desk, chairs, sideboard, wall paneling—was dark, gleaming wood, masculine and somber. There were a couple of framed paintings, also dark toned, and some framed documents that looked to be copies of his law degrees. A big polished silver golf trophy reared up on a shelf above the sideboard.

Mantle indicated a chair in front of the desk, went around, and sat down in a big leather chair behind it. He folded his thick hands together on the blotter and sat statue stiff, studying her some more with those stern eyes. Not saying anything, waiting for her lead.

She didn't waste any time. "Lucas Zeller," she said, "isn't who he claims to be. His real name's Delman, Antoine Delman. And his business isn't investments; it's petty theft and con games."

Nothing changed in the judge's expression. He still didn't say anything, just kept looking at her. Hadn't blinked even once since they'd sat down. She wondered if he was trying to quietly intimidate her. Wasn't working, if that was it. She'd grown up with Pop's stares and glares; the hard eye didn't phase her anymore.

She said, "He doesn't work alone. Has himself a partner—his mother. Her name is Alisha Delman."

That got a couple of blinks out of Mantle. "Alisha?"

"As in 'Psychic Readings by Alisha.' That's her specialty—posing as a psychic to help set up marks."

Silent stare. Mr. Stone Face.

"They both spent a couple of years in prison," Tamara said, "for running a con in Southern California—bilking black investors in a charity scam. A fund that was supposed to help struggling African American families keep their homes. The investors put up the cash and take a tax write-off; the families pay back the money at a reasonable interest rate, everybody makes out. Only the fund doesn't exist and the only folks who make out, if they don't get caught, are the Delmans—they disappear with the investment capital. Sound familiar, Your Honor?"

The stony look.

"Operation Save is their new con," she said. "More sophisticated than the one they worked down south. They set up a Web site this time, desktop-published some brochures with fake quotes and statistics. I'll bet you looked at the Web site but didn't investigate Operation Save any further than that. Am I right?"

More silence. She let it go on, let him be the one to break it. Took more than a minute. His lips barely moved when he said, "How do you know all this?"

"It's my business."

"You seem to believe it's mine as well."

"No, I meant the business I'm in. The detective business."

"That doesn't answer my question. Who hired you?"

"I can't tell you that. Privileged."

"Stop playing games with me, young woman. Tell me what makes you think I'm associated in any way with Lucas Zeller."

"Antoine Delman," Tamara said. "And I don't think it; I know it."

"What do you know?"

"That he and Alisha are behind Operation Save. That he's been working on you and Doctor Easy to invest—others, too, probably. And that his mother's been working on Viveca Inman."

"Am I supposed to know these people you're talking about?"

"Come on, Judge, you were with Hawkins last night at the Twilight Lounge on Ocean. And you were driving the BMW you just bought from Mrs. Inman."

The look. Seemed like you couldn't crack it if you used a hammer.

Finally he said, "You were there and you followed me," in the same tone you'd use to talk about the weather. Statement, not a question.

"Straight to Psychic Readings by Alisha," Tamara said. "You drove Mrs. Inman there, went to the Twilight meeting and then back afterward to pick her up. Got together with her to decide whether or not to invest in the O.S. Fund. Right?"

Mantle didn't answer. He seemed to be thinking on something else. He said, "How did you—," and then stopped, and moved for the first time since he'd sat down: his hands unlocked and he spread them out flat on the desktop. "Stewart," he said then. "Deron Stewart."

Her turn to be silent.

"He's another one like you," the judge said flatly. "A paid snoop."

"Operative." No reason not to admit it. There wasn't any need now for Stewart to keep working undercover. "That's right; he is."

"Why? Why the deception?"

"To find Antoine Delman."

"And what other purpose?"

"No other purpose."

"I don't believe you. You know what Stewart knows."

Be straight with the man, she thought. Always the best way to go, and besides, it'd give her a certain amount of leverage. "About the club. Yes."

"The club," he said in that talking-about-the-weather tone again. "Tell me how you found out about it."

"I knew Delman was on the down low, never mind how."

"I don't like that term."

"Okay, then I won't use it again."

"How many people have you told about the club?"

"None except Stewart. And I guarantee he won't repeat it."

Another long silence. Then, "Do you realize how serious a crime blackmail is, Ms. Corbin?"

"Blackmail? That what you think I'm here for?"

"Well?"

"You couldn't be more wrong," Tamara said. "My agency has one of the best reps in the city."

Silence.

"I don't care what you do in private, Judge. Or what any consenting adults do in private. None of my business. Believe it."

"Why are you here, then?"

"To save you and Mrs. Inman and Doctor Easy and anybody else who's thinking of investing in Operation Save from being ripped off. Call it my Operation Save."

"Very noble of you."

"I'm not trying to be noble. Like I said before—"

"*As* I said before."

She almost smiled. Correcting her grammar in the middle of a conversation like this. Judge Mantle was some piece of work.

"*As* I said before, I'm trying to put Antoine Delman and his mother behind bars where they belong."

Another silence, a short one this time. "Do you have proof they're who and what you claim?"

"Enough to be sure I'm right about them and Operation Save."

"Then why haven't you gone to the police? Or have you?"

"Not yet. The one thing I don't know for sure is whether or not any money has changed hands. The Delmans' scam doesn't become a felony until that happens."

"You don't need to explain the law to me, Ms. Corbin."

"*Has* any money changed hands, far as you know?"

Mantle said carefully, "It's my understanding that some investments in the charity have been made."

"By anyone you know personally?"

"Yes."

"Who? Doctor Easy?"

"Yes."

"How much were you planning to invest?"

The look. She thought he was going to stonewall the question, but he didn't. He said, "Twenty-five thousand dollars."

"Mrs. Inman?"

"The same."

"Doctor Easy?"

"Thirty thousand."

"Cash?"

"There was never any mention of cash."

"Doesn't need to be on this kind of scam. Cashier's checks are just as good. Even personal checks, if they're guaranteed to clear right away."

Silence.

"Delman been pressuring you and Mrs. Inman to invest?"

"Not exactly."

Uh-huh. The soft sell, while Alisha worked on her. "Delman steered you to Alisha when he found out Mrs. Inman was into psychics, right?"

"He gave me her name, yes."

"And you've been waiting for Mrs. Inman to make up her mind. If she decides to go ahead, so do you."

"Yes."

"You believe in psychics, too, Judge?"

Silence.

"Has Mrs. Inman made up her mind?"

"Yes."

"Going ahead?"

"Yes."

"When? How soon?"

"Next Monday. At her home."

"So there's plenty of time for the SFPD to set up a sting. All we have to do—"

"We? You expect me to go to the police with you?"

"Somebody has to."

"And you picked me. Do you have any idea what the publicity on something like this could do to my reputation, my career on the bench, my marriage?"

"How can it hurt you? You're a *potential* victim, that's all. All you've done is consider an investment in what you believed was a legitimate charity."

"That's not what concerns me," Mantle said.

"No? Oh . . . the club."

"That's right, the club."

"None of that has to come out—"

"Unless Delman brings it out. Or it comes out some other way."

"Well, that's a risk whether you go in with me or not. The Delmans are going down, one way or another—I promise you that. Do us all a favor and help me bust them."

"And if I refuse?"

"Then I'll have to talk to Mrs. Inman," Tamara said. "Tell her I went to you first and you turned me down. And tell the police the same thing."

Mantle deliberated again. Somewhere in the house a clock bonged; it was so quiet Tamara could hear the faint after-echoes.

He said finally, "It's my place to discuss this business with Mrs. Inman, not yours. Dr. Hawkins as well. They have a right to know the situation before I agree to do anything."

"That's fair. Maybe you could convince them to go in, too. The more witnesses, the better."

"They may want their names kept out of it, if possible."

"But you'll come with me in any case? If I have to go in alone, I won't keep anybody's name out of it."

"You seem to have left me no choice."

"Can you talk to them tonight?"

"Not Mrs. Inman. She's attending a charity benefit in San Jose. Sometime tomorrow. That should be soon enough to suit you."

"You don't sound very grateful, Judge."

"It remains to be seen if I have anything to be grateful for."

Tamara laid one of her business cards on the desk in front of him. "You can reach me at one of those numbers anytime. The sooner the better, okay? For everybody's sake."

Mantle didn't answer. Didn't say another word to her. Just got up and looked at her until she did the same, then ushered her out into the cold night.

22

The owner of the old two-toned van and the DDTDAWG license plate was an ex-con named Joseph Hoffman.

Tamara got me that information on Thursday morning. She also tracked down Hoffman's felony record. The crime that had landed him in Folsom for twenty-seven months had nothing to do with drugs and was the only blot on his record: receiving and selling stolen property. He'd owned a junk shop out near the Cow Palace, and when the cops raided it they found a storeroom full of small appliances, computers, and other goods taken in various burglaries throughout the city. He claimed he hadn't known any of the stuff was hot; the judge and jury didn't believe him. His sentence had been three years, with time knocked off for good behavior. Since his release eighteen months ago, he'd been living in Daly City, working for a reputable salvage dealer in South San Francisco, and apparently avoiding any further trouble with the law.

Nothing in any of that to tie him to a middle school teacher like Zachary Ullman, at least on the surface. There was one potentially interesting fact: the police had found out about Hoffman's fencing operation not on their own hook but through a tip from a source so reliable that they'd had no trouble getting a search warrant for the premises raid.

The tipster had been Hoffman's wife, Rosette.

She'd also testified against him at his trial, claiming she'd discovered what he was up to by accident and felt it her duty to "do the right thing" and turn him in. The last honest citizen. But there were other motivations in such cases. One possibility was that she'd known about the fencing or suspected it all along, the marriage had turned rocky, and she'd made up her mind to throw Hubby to the wolves. Another was payback for some offense other than a failing marriage. A third was sheer malice. In any case, she'd divorced Hoffman immediately after he was convicted, taken her seven-year-old son and her share from the sale of the junk shop, and started a new life under her maiden name, Prescott. Current address: 1499 Javon Street, El Cerrito. Current place of employment: Sweet Treats Bakery, Fairmount Avenue, El Cerrito.

She was the person to talk to. Nobody knows a man better than his ex-wife, or is more likely to dish up any dirt she has on him when the relationship ends badly. And that went double for an ex-wife who'd already been instrumental in putting her former hubby away in the slam for twenty-seven months.

Sweet Treats Bakery was located at the outer edge of a massive shopping center that took up three or four blocks along San Pablo and Fairmount avenues. One of those places that dispense coffee and other beverages along with cakes, cookies, pies, fresh breads: windowed display cases and a counter along one wall, a few tables and chairs occupying the rest of the space.

I can't walk into a bakery without two things happening: the aromas make my mouth water and my stomach growl, and my nostalgia gene kicks in. Bakeries were a consistent draw when I was a kid in the Outer Mission. One in particular, an Italian place near where we lived that specialized in sourdough, focaccia, Pugliese, and anise Easter breads and Ligurian pastries. Nobody who grew up with those aromas in his nostrils can recall them without drooling.

The smells in Sweet Treats were mild by comparison, but even with the Ullman business weighing on my mind, the saliva juices flowed. I hadn't been hungry this morning, had settled for coffee and a soft-boiled egg before leaving the condo, and I hadn't had any lunch yet. I wondered if they had Pugliese and if they did, if it was up to my standards. I can eat half a loaf of good Pugliese, warm, without butter or any other topping. Kerry was always after me to limit my carb intake, and usually I obliged her for the sake of my waistline. But Pugliese . . .

The lunch trade had thinned out and only a couple of the tables were occupied. Two women worked the counter, both around forty, one thin and henna haired, one fat and dishwater blond. The thin one was waiting on a customer. The fat one stood by herself at the other end refilling one of the coffeemakers, so I went down there and smiled at her and asked if she was Rosette Prescott.

She'd put on a smile in response to mine; it turned upside down at the sound of her name. "Yes, that's me." Tired voice, tired eyes—the kind of tiredness that has little to do with physical fatigue. Weltschmerz.

"Could we talk privately for a few minutes? A personal matter."

She glanced over at the thin woman, then out at the remaining customers, before she leaned forward and said in an undertone, "Look, if you're here about the car payments, I—"

"No, nothing like that. It's about your ex-husband."

She had a round, soft, pale face, like well-kneaded bread dough, but when I said "ex-husband" it reshaped into hard, bitter lines. The hardness and bitterness were in her voice, too: "What about him? Who are you?"

I showed her my license, holding the case up against my chest and shielding it with my body so only she could see it. "He's involved in a case I'm investigating."

"I don't care what he's involved in."

"But I do, Ms. Prescott. The case is personal."

"What do you mean, personal?"

"It concerns one of my family members."

She hesitated, glancing again at her co-worker. "If you're gonna make me have anything to do with him, the answer is no."

"Just a few questions, that's all. You'll never see me again afterward."

"Or him?"

"Or him. He'll never know we talked."

"What you want to know . . . will it get him in trouble? The kind of trouble he was in before, or some other kind?"

"It might."

"Then all right." She went over to the henna-haired woman, said something to her that evoked a brief argument. When Rosette came back to where I waited, she made a *follow me* gesture and waddled through a swing door behind the counter.

I stepped around and through into a big, empty bakery kitchen. Open at the far end was a cell-like enclosure, what's called a break room—a table, a couple of chairs, a small refrigerator. She sank heavily into one of the chairs, puffing a little, and leaned forward to rub one of her thick ankles.

"I wasn't always this fat," she said. "Big, but not fat. He made me this way. Joe, that son of a bitch. Just one more thing he did to me."

"An abuser?"

"He never hit me, if that's what you mean. But you don't have to hit somebody to beat them up and beat them down."

"No," I said, "you don't."

"He tried to do the same thing to our boy. You know I have a son?"

"Yes."

"Chuck. He's nine now. I got him away from Joe in time, I think. He's doing okay in school; he don't act out like he used to. He won't grow up to be like his father, not if I can help it. He—" She broke off, flapped one hand in a weary way. "You don't want to hear all this. And I can't take more than ten minutes or Connie'll throw a fit; it's almost time for her break. Ask your questions."

"You may have already answered one of them—why you turned your husband in to the police four years ago. Because of the way he treated you and your son?"

"No. That wasn't the reason."

"Did it have anything to do with drugs?"

"Drugs? No, he never had nothing to do with that crap; I'll give him that much."

"Duty, then? Moral reasons?"

"Duty's what I said at the trial, that I did it on account of I found out about the stolen property and it wasn't right to let him get away with it. I couldn't tell nobody the real reason. I wanted to, I wanted to tell the cops when I turned him in, but I didn't have no proof. Not anymore. My own damn fault."

"Proof of what?"

Flesh rippled as she shook her head. Not in response to my question, at her bitter memories. "It would've been my word against his and they couldn't have done anything to him. And I didn't want Chuck to know, nobody to know, what kind of man I was married to. Stupid. I was so damn mad when I found out . . . I went a little crazy, you know? Got rid of it, burned it all up."

"You're not talking about the stolen property. . . ."

"No, I knew about that already. Well, I didn't really know; I didn't *want* to know where the money was coming from. We were living pretty good, Chuck didn't want for nothing except a decent father. No, it wasn't that." Her mouth thinned down until it resembled a knife slice in her doughy face. "It was the other goddamn thing."

"What other thing, Ms. Prescott?"

She told me.

And all the good, warm bakery smells suddenly turned rancid.

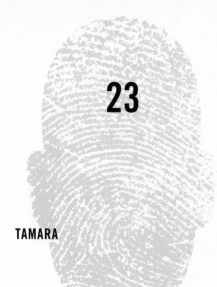

23

TAMARA

More waiting.

All day long she waited.

Time seemed to contract, slow way down, as it had in high school before she found out how good she was with computers. Kept busy but still found herself clock-watching. And jumping a little every time the phone rang. But none of the callers was Judge Mantle.

She did some work for Bill—a license plate check with the DMV that produced another yelp of protest from Marjorie, plus a deep b.g. search on the owner of the car. The name and info didn't fit any of the agency cases. Something to do with Emily's middle school teacher, maybe, and what was up with that? Bill didn't want to talk about it, any more than she did about the Delmans and Operation Save. Secrets. The serious personal kind for him, too.

Jake Runyon came in with a report on the Madison bail-jump case. Closed, but with an unexpected twist to what had seemed a routine investigation. Reading Jake's report, she realized she hadn't paid enough attention to the agency caseload the past couple of weeks. Too much on her mind, too much focus on nailing Antoine and Alisha. But that was no excuse for leaving contract work undone or giving it short shrift. Business to run here. She hadn't even gotten around to the monthly billing yet.

She attacked the backlog, and that helped make the time go by a little faster. Not much faster, though. Not fast enough.

Noon hour came and went. Tamara worked right through it. Wasn't hungry; too tensed up, waiting for the judge's call.

And it kept not coming.

One o'clock. Two o'clock. Three calls, none from Mantle.

Why? Hadn't been able to get in touch with Viveca Inman? Still deliberating? Decided not to cooperate and was blowing her off? No, he wouldn't do that—just blow her off. He knew she'd go to the cops without his cooperation if he forced her to. She was pretty good at reading people; Mantle wasn't the kind of man to stick his head in the sand and hope it'd all go away. Whatever he decided, he'd call and tell her.

So why the hell didn't he?

Three o'clock. Still nothing.

Tamara got on the horn herself then. Found out from the judge's aide at City Hall that he wasn't on the bench or in chambers. He'd been in court this morning but then canceled his afternoon session and left "on personal business."

Home by now? No. The woman who answered the phone said he wasn't there and she didn't know when he would be; she'd expected him to be in court all day.

Four o'clock. No word.

Five o'clock. No word.

Now Tamara was really wired. Shouldn't be letting the delay affect her the way it was—a few more hours, even another day, wouldn't make any difference. But damn, when you were close like this, when you wanted something as badly as she wanted Antoine and Alisha put away, all the waiting around couldn't help but work on your nerves.

Keep on hanging here or close up and go home? Her home and cell numbers, as well as the agency's, were on the card she'd given the judge; he could reach her no matter where she was. Give it another hour, she thought—but all she was able to stand was another ten minutes. Stay in the office any longer and she'd start bouncing off the walls. New Olympic gymnastic event: wall-bouncing. Get herself started and she'd be a prime candidate for the gold.

She locked the agency, ransomed her car from the parking garage. The Toyota's engine was starting to make funny pinging noises. Horace's hand-me-down had better not give her any trouble before she traded it in. Should've gotten rid of it weeks ago, when she'd moved out of the Sunset District apartment they'd shared, into her new flat on Potrero Hill. Promised herself she would, and probably would've if she hadn't let that son of a bitch Lucas . . . Antoine . . . crawl into her life. First thing she'd do when this business was finished was dump that sucker and buy herself the best ride she could afford.

The new crib was the entire second floor of a refurbished Stick Victorian on Connecticut Street, easily the nicest place she'd ever lived in the city. She'd only had it a little over a month, and with her life in upheaval the past three weeks there'd hardly been time for her to settle in. Still a stack of un-packed boxes to deal with, still some painting and other work to be done, before she could really start enjoying the place.

As soon as she came in she checked her answering machine. No messages—not that that was surprising. Almost never were anymore; if somebody wanted to leave a phone message for her, they called the agency or went to her cell's voice mail. The answering machine was something else she might as well get rid of. The landline, too, while she was at it. You just didn't need either of them anymore these days.

In the kitchen she poured herself a glass of merlot to try to unwind a little. The prospect of sitting around all evening, waiting for the judge to call, really would have her wall-bouncing. If she didn't hear from him by seven thirty, she'd drive over to Monterey Heights and hope to surprise him at home.

She'd just sat down in the living room, taken her first sip of wine, when the doorbell went off.

Now who the hell was that? Not Vonda or any of her other friends; they never dropped over unannounced. You got solicitors in the evenings here sometimes—salesmen and political and religious prosletyzers. Well, she'd make short work of whoever it was. She was in no mood to talk to anybody tonight except Judge Alfred Mantle.

The Victorian's owners hadn't bothered to have a communicator or door buzzer installed when they renovated it, so you had to go all the way down the inside stairs to find out who was ringing the bell. No problem if it was somebody you wanted to see, but an irritation if it wasn't. Well, it was a minor inconvenience. Everything else about the flat made it worth the high rent she was paying.

She hadn't put the chain on the door when she came in, didn't think to put it on before she threw the dead bolt and opened up. Mistake—big mistake.

Soon as she turned the knob, a heavy weight slammed against the panel and drove it straight back into her face. Pain erupted, blood spurted from her nose, and the force of the blow sent her staggering backward along the short hall to the foot of the stairs. Her heel stubbed against the bottom riser. And down she went against the stairs, another of the risers jamming hard into her back, the impact taking some of her breath away.

Dimly, through a haze of hurt, she saw Antoine Delman come inside and push the door closed behind him, throw the dead bolt to lock it. Then he was standing over her, a smile like a rictus on his ugly, blocky face.

"Hello, Tamara," he said. "Hello, you fucking bitch."

24

JAKE RUNYON

He had two calls that afternoon on his way back to the agency from an interview on the new case Tamara had given him, a skip-trace for a prominent S.F. couple whose daughter had disappeared. The first call was from Bryn—something of a surprise, since it came during working hours. She seldom called him at all, letting him take the initiative, and never until after five o'clock.

"Jake, I'm sorry to bother you like this; I know you're busy—"

"Not a problem. What's up?"

"I know we said tomorrow night, but . . . could you come over tonight instead?"

There was a strained quality to her voice that made him ask, "Something wrong?"

". . . Yes. Something that happened today."

"What? You okay?"

"Yes. I don't want to talk about it on the phone. Can you come over?"

"Right away, if it's urgent."

"No, tonight's soon enough."

"You sure?"

"I'm sure. Any time you can make it."

New development with her health, the facial paralysis? He hoped that wasn't it; it probably wouldn't be good news if it was. Support or custody troubles with the ex-husband? No use speculating. He'd find out soon enough.

But he was still wondering when the second call came in. Bill, this time. And he didn't sound any better than Bryn had. Even more tense; his voice was as tight and flat as Runyon had ever heard it.

"Jake, I need to talk to you—in person. You busy?"

"On my way back to the agency."

"Where are you?"

"Just leaving St. Francis Wood."

"When you get to South Park, don't wait for me in the office—meet me in the South Park Café. I'm in the East Bay, heading for the Bay Bridge. I shouldn't be far behind you."

"Business you don't want Tamara to know about?"

"Business I don't want anybody to know about except you. Not yet."

The South Park Café was mid-afternoon quiet, only a handful of customers taking up bar space. Runyon ordered draft beer, took it to the table farthest removed from any of the other occupied ones. He was still nursing it when Bill walked in fifteen minutes later.

As soon as he sat down, Runyon could see how tensed up the man was. Holding in whatever was bugging him as if it were an explosive that might go off at any second. When Runyon raised the beer glass Bill shook his head, leaned forward with both hands flat on the table.

"I'm going to ask a favor," Bill said, "but I won't hold it against you if you say no."

"Why would I say no?"

"What I want you to do could have a backlash."

"What kind of backlash?"

"The kind that could get us and the agency in trouble. That's one reason I don't want Tamara to know about it yet."

"Trouble with the law?"

"Potentially. Could put our licenses in jeopardy. I don't think that'll happen, but it could if I'm off base here."

"But you're pretty sure you're not."

"Pretty sure," Bill said. "But not a hundred percent. It's going to take a little muscle to find out for certain."

"How much muscle?"

"Nothing heavy. Just enough to get inside a guy's house."

"Hard guy?"

"No. And no family, lives alone."

"Unlawful entry, then. That the backlash you mean?"

"That's it."

"I've run that risk before," Runyon said. "We both have. This is important to you, right? Personal?"

"Yeah. Personal."

"And you want me along why? Not for extra muscle, if the guy isn't a hardcase. Intimidation? Witness?"

"They're part of the reason."

"What's the other part?"

Bill said grimly, "If I'm right, to keep me from doing something I might regret for the rest of my life."

· · ·

Zachary Ullman wasn't home.

No lights, no car in the driveway, no answer to the doorbell.

They sat waiting in Runyon's Ford, parked a few doors up-street. Neither of them said anything. Bill had laid it all out for him in the South Park Café and they'd talked it over a little more on the drive out here to Daly City. Nothing to do now but wait.

Gray daylight began to fade; fog came pouring in in humped white waves, like an avalanche in slow motion. Ragged stream-ers of mist broke loose from the mass overhead, curled down along the twisty street, thickening slowly until the shapes of the houses beyond the curve ahead lost definition. Night shadows formed and spread and lights bloomed in windows. More cars rolled by in both directions—residents coming home from work—but none of them turned into Ullman's driveway.

Waiting like this didn't bother Runyon. He sat with his mind cranked down to basic awareness, a trick he'd learned on stakeouts in Seattle and honed fine during Colleen's long, slow cancer death. It wasn't a matter of maintaining patience; it was a way to keep from thinking about things like pain and suffering and grief, things that could drive you up to the edge if you let yourself dwell on them.

Bill hadn't learned the trick. He was always fidgety on stakeouts and worse when he was stressed this way—thinking too much, letting his thoughts and emotions run unchecked. He kept shifting around on the seat, blowing out heavy breaths, doing things with his hands and feet. Once he mut-tered, "Come on, come on, come *on!*" Runyon didn't blame him. Even if Bill was wrong about what he expected to find in Ullman's house, there was still the cocaine Emily had picked up. That was enough cause and justification right there for what they were going to do.

Not easy being a father. Runyon hadn't been much of a one to Joshua, but that hadn't been his fault; Andrea, with her booze-fueled bitterness and hatred, hadn't given him an opportunity. But he had the parental gene; he understood what Bill was going through, why he didn't trust himself to brace Ullman alone tonight. If their situations were reversed, he might not be so calm sitting here, either.

Full dark now. Getting on toward six o'clock. No telling when Ullman would finally show up; if he'd gone out to dinner or a show or a meeting of some kind, they could be here for hours. Pretty soon he'd have to call Bryn, tell her he'd be late, might not be able to make it at all tonight. Better do it now, get it over with—

No.

Headlights crawling toward them through the mist, slowing, turning into Ullman's driveway.

Bill laid fingers like steel bands on Runyon's arm. "That's him."

"Can't make out if he's alone."

"Not yet."

The garage door rolled up down there. Enough light from inside spilled out for a clearer view of the car—a light-colored compact—and the shadowed interior.

"He's alone," Bill said.

The car disappeared inside the garage; the door rolled down again.

Runyon asked, "How much time do we give him?"

"Enough to get inside the house. We move as soon as a light goes on."

It didn't take much more than a minute. The instant the front window became a pale yellow rectangle, they were out of the car.

Fast walk across the street, up the front path—careful not to make any noise as they climbed to the door. Bill leaned on the bell, kept his finger on it. Footsteps. And a voice said, "Who is it? Who's out there?"

Bill glanced at Runyon, shook his head. He jabbed the bell again.

"I said who's out there?"

And again.

Rattle of a dead-bolt lock. Runyon stepped aside, into the heavy shadows, so he couldn't be seen when the door opened partway on a chain.

"You again. What's the idea of ringing my bell like that—"

Bill said, "Let me in, Ullman. I want to talk to you."

"No. I have nothing to say to you. Go away."

"I'm coming in, one way or another."

"No, you're not—"

Ullman tried to close the door. Bill jammed his body against it, and Runyon crowded in next to him to help hold it open. A bleated "No!" from inside. B & E if they busted the chain . . . and the hell with it. Their combined weight shoved it taut, snapped the plate loose on the second push; the door flew inward, the knob banging loudly off the inner wall.

Bill shoved in after it. Over his shoulder Runyon saw Ullman's slight figure backing away with his hands up in front of him, his narrow face pinched white with fear.

"Two of you! My God, what's the idea, what do you want? I'll call the police—"

Bill said, "You won't call anybody."

"Are you here to beat me up? Is that what—"

"Shut up. Just stand still and be quiet, don't give me an excuse."

They crowded Ullman down a long hallway that opened into a smallish living room at the rear. Nothing special about it—nondescript furniture except for a long oak sideboard, a flat-screen TV, three cases stuffed with books. Bill went to the sideboard, opened doors to look inside. Runyon moved to the bookcases, scanned the spines of a mix of hardcovers and trade paperbacks. Science and history subjects, mostly, and a smattering of classical fiction.

"Nothing," he said.

"Nothing here, either."

"Oh my God," Ullman said, "what're you *looking* for?" He was so scared now he was shaking visibly.

"You know the answer to that."

"No. No . . ."

Dining room next, with Ullman stumbling along behind them. Nothing. Kitchen. Nothing. Down a short cross-hallway to the first of three closed doors, probably a bedroom.

"*No!*" Ullman screamed the word this time. "Don't go in there; you can't go in there!"

Bill pulled the door open and Runyon followed him in.

Bedroom, all right. But like no bedroom Runyon had ever seen or wanted to see again. Bill had been right, dead right. It was all there—all the proof he or the law would ever need. On the dresser and the bedside table, in another bookcase, no doubt on the computer that sat on a trestle desk. And on the walls. Jesus, especially on the walls.

Child porn.

The worst, the sickest imaginable.

This wasn't just a bedroom; it was a goddamned filthy shrine.

25

The photographs were the worst.

There were seven or eight of them, all in color and hideously graphic, a couple blown up to the size of small posters. Grown men with both girls and boys, the youngest six or seven, the oldest Emily's age. Entangled bodies and leering male faces. Images to make you puke. And there'd be more, a lot more, on Ullman's computer and the VHS tapes and stacks of scrapbooks in the bookcase. He wasn't just a sick son of a bitch who got off on kiddie porn; he was archiving the stuff with the aid of Joe Hoffman and others like him.

I couldn't keep looking at those photographs; just the few random glances made my eyeballs feel seared. A low keening sound shifted my gaze toward the doorway. Ullman was slumped against the jamb, hanging on to it with both hands, tears leaking out of his haunted eyes. I've only hated one man as much as I hated him in that moment, and I'd been responsible for that man's death. I had vowed never to let anything like that happen again, but it took effort to beat down a savage urge to hurt Zachary Ullman. Hurt him bad. If I hadn't brought Jake along . . .

I quit looking at Ullman. The desk was in my line of sight

then, and on it next to the laptop computer was a bronze-colored, rough-textured tin box about three sizes larger than the one Emily had found and brought home—part of a set. I went over there, worked the lid up.

Runyon said, "What's in there?"

"His cocaine stash. Full Baggie."

"One more charge against— Bill!"

I swung around. Ullman was no longer hugging the jamb; the doorway was empty.

Runyon ducked into the hallway with me close behind. Ullman had made it into the living room by then—I could hear him bang into something in there. But he wasn't trying to get out of the house, wasn't anywhere near the front door. He was hunched at an end table next to a recliner, clawing open its single drawer.

I yelled his name and Runyon made a lunge in his direction. Too late. Ullman straightened, pivoting, and he had a gun in his hand.

"Stay away! Don't come any closer!"

Runyon pulled up short. So did I. We'd both missed the gun in the quick search earlier, too intent on hunting for the child porn. Hadn't occurred to either of us that Ullman might have one, and it should have—Christ, it should have. The piece was a small-caliber automatic and he wasn't just holding it; he was waving it wildly in front of him in a hand that trembled like somebody afflicted with Parkinson's. The wildness was in his eyes, too; they bulged as if they might pop from the pressure.

I said, "Put it down, Ullman. Don't make things any worse for yourself."

"No! I don't want to shoot you, but I will if you try to stop me. I will!"

"You can't run," Runyon said. "How far do you think you'd get?"

"Stay where you are, don't come near me."

He backed away from the recliner. We were between him and the front door, but he wasn't going that way. He kept backing, waggling that damn gun, into the dining room, where he bumped into a chair and almost knocked it over. He didn't seem to notice, just kept on backing.

The kitchen, I thought. That was where the door to the garage was.

Runyon and I were up on the balls of our feet, leaning forward a little, like sprinters waiting in the blocks. Ullman was halfway across the dining room now. Two more steps and he'd be into the kitchen, out of our sight. One more—

Go!

Him running in the kitchen, us running crouched through the dining room. Runyon, younger and faster, was ahead of me when we neared the kitchen arch. From there I could see Ullman at the garage door, yanking it open. He jabbed the automatic in our direction and we both ducked aside reflexively, but he didn't fire. He plunged through, slammed the door behind him.

We were there in a couple of seconds, but when Runyon grabbed the knob it bound up in his hand. He said, "Snap lock. Won't take long to break it."

"I'll try to stop him out front. Careful, Jake—don't go up against that gun."

He didn't answer.

I ran back into the living room. There was a brass urn on a stand against one wall; I grabbed it on the way by. Not much of a weapon, but I had to have something. I could hear Runyon working on the door in the kitchen, thought I heard the lock snap free before I went charging outside.

Down the steps in three quick jumps, across a strip of lawn to the garage. The door was still all the way down and I didn't hear anything to indicate it was about to come up. I stopped and stood there breathing hard, the brass urn slick in my fingers, while thirty seconds, a minute, ticked away and the foggy cold dried the sweat on me and made me shiver. Sounds filtered out from inside, faint, unidentifiable. None of them was the rumble of a car engine; I'd've been able to hear that clearly enough. What the hell was happening in there?

Another few seconds and I found out. The automatic opener finally whirred and the door began to slide up. There was plenty of light inside—the overheads were on. I took a firmer grip on the urn, set myself, and bent to look under the bottom edge.

Ullman's Hyundai was sitting there dark and silent.

Then, as the door ground all the way up, I saw Runyon standing next to the car, the driver's door wide open and Ullman unmoving inside. The little automatic was in Runyon's hand; he semaphored it over his head to let me know he had it.

I let out a heavy breath, set the urn down, and went in there. Ullman was sitting with both hands on the steering wheel. All the wildness was gone; so were the tears. His eyes no longer bulged, didn't even blink. His face was a literal mask of misery. Not self-pity—raw, naked misery.

I said to Runyon, "What happened?"

"He wasn't trying to run. He came out here to kill himself."

"I couldn't do it," Ullman said in an empty voice. "I thought this time I could, now finally I could, but I couldn't. I can't. I'm too much of a coward."

"You're a hell of a lot worse than that."

"I know," he said. "Don't you think I know what I am?"

Runyon said, "He had the piece to his temple when I got in here. Just kept holding it there, didn't move when I took it away from him. Took me a minute to find the door opener."

"Let's get him inside."

Ullman said, "Why don't you just kill me? Couldn't you do that? Make it look like I killed myself?"

"You're not going to get off that easy."

"I'd rather die than go to prison. I want to die. I ache to die."

Runyon and I traded glances. Somebody might accommodate Ullman someday in whatever prison facility he ended up in. Child molesters and child porn addicts were bottom of the barrel inside the walls, primary targets for con vengeance.

We dragged Ullman out of the car and back into the house, sat him down on the living room couch. While I called the Daly City cops and told them what we had, Runyon went to close the front door; I'd left it wide open. He bent to look at the hanging chain plate, beckoned me over when I was done with the call.

"Plate tore out clean," he said. "I think I can screw it back in so the damage won't show."

"I doubt that it matters now."

"Why don't I do it anyway." He got out one of those multi-bladed pocketknives and went to work with the screwdriver blade.

I took up a stand in front of Ullman. The way he was sitting, motionless, the haunted eyes staring out from under drooping lids, he might have been a propped-up cadaver. His face was corpselike, too: the color and consistency of white wax inlaid with filaments of blood.

"I know you hate me," he said, his mouth barely moving, "and I don't blame you. But you can't possibly hate me as much as I hate myself."

I didn't say anything.

"Every day for the past fifteen years, loathing myself. Do you know how many times I tried to put a bullet through my head? Dozens. Literally dozens. I came close once, but at the last second I couldn't do it. I'm too much of a coward."

"You said that before."

The words kept running out of him in a hushed, barren voice, almost a whisper, as if he were confessing cardinal sins to a priest. "Cowardice and self-hatred. That's why I started using cocaine. I thought that if I got high enough, I could pull the trigger or swallow pills or poison . . . something, anything, to end it. But all the cocaine did was make me hate myself a little less. And after a while it had the opposite effect. It made the sickness worse, the cravings even more intense."

The taste of bile was in my mouth. I wanted to spit, swallowed instead.

"I'm sorry about Emily," he said.

"Don't talk to me about my daughter. Don't say her name."

"She found the little box in the school parking lot. I don't know how I could have lost it; I was always so careful. Maybe I lost it on purpose, subconsciously; I don't know. I was terrified when she came to me, told me she'd found it and took it home . . . terrified when you came here last night. But not anymore. Now I'm glad. I'm glad it's almost over."

He fell silent. The silence lasted long enough for me to think he'd run out of words, but he hadn't. Not quite.

"There's something else I have to say, something I want you to know."

"I don't want to hear it," I said. "Save it for the police and your lawyer."

"I never hurt a child, never touched a child. Never. Never wanted to. It was the looking I needed, that's all. Looking. Looking."

"We both know that's a lie, Ullman. Men like you always want to do more than look, whether you act on the impulses or not. The only thing that stopped you was fear of getting caught."

"No—"

"Your students, my daughter, every child you taught or came in contact with, you imagined up there on that bedroom wall. And not with some other pervert—with you. Always with *you*."

He stared straight ahead for a few seconds. Then, slowly, he lifted one hand and passed it down over his face, and when it dropped into his lap his eyes were closed—the same gesture you'd use to close the eyes of a corpse.

Zachary Ullman may not have had the guts to shoot or poison himself, but he was dead just the same. And had been for a long time.

Dead man breathing.

26

TAMARA

The funny thing was, she wasn't afraid.

There she was, sprawled out on the floor against the stairs with her skirt hiked up around her ass, blood leaking out of her nose and pain pulsing through her, and all she felt was rage. Even when Delman took the switch knife out of his pocket and snicked it open, the thin curls of fear that rose in her burned away almost immediately, like paper on a hot fire.

He takes another step, she thought, I'll kick him in the balls. Squash 'em like grapes until the juice runs out.

But he didn't take another step. He said, "You just couldn't leave it alone, could you?" The smile that wasn't a smile was gone now. His mouth was hard, bent out of shape with a fury that matched hers. Hate radiated off of him; you could almost see the shimmers. "Had to come after me and my mother, lay some hurt on us. Well, now it's your turn, baby. Now you're getting the hurt laid on you."

She sucked air through her mouth, struggled to sit up on the bottom stair riser. Her nose felt swollen, big as a balloon, numb. Blood dribbled into her mouth; she pawed and spat it away. The whole front of her blouse was splattered with it.

"Don't even think about screaming," he said. "You do and I'll stick you like the pig you are."

Screaming wouldn't do her any good anyway. Her downstairs neighbors, white couple, the Jastrows, both worked late jobs that didn't get them home until after eight. She said, in a voice that didn't sound like hers, thick and nasal, "Murder's not your thing, Antoine."

"Don't bet on it." Then, "Antoine. Shit." Then, "Best deal we ever had going, six-figure payoff. Clean, smooth, and you fucked it up. You're going to pay for that, Tamara."

"How? Cut me up? Beat me up?"

"You'll find out."

"Your mama know you're here?"

"Shut up about my mother."

"No, she doesn't know. Your idea. She won't like it when she finds out."

"Get up off the floor."

"Why don't you come down here with me?"

"Smart-mouth bitch." He kicked her ankle, kicked her again above the knee, hard enough to make her grimace and clamp her teeth. "Get up off the goddamn floor!"

Tamara pulled her skirt down, managed to turn onto her hip, then onto her knees facing the side wall. It took a little effort, one hand on the wall and the other on the railing, to get onto her feet. Her breathing still wasn't right. Air made whistling, wheezing sounds in her nasal passages.

He gestured with the knife. "Upstairs."

Her legs felt wobbly; she had to hang on to the railing with both hands to make the climb. Didn't do it fast enough to suit him. Twice he jabbed fingers into her back, the second time on the spot where the riser had cut into her back. She swallowed the pain cry that rose into her throat. Wouldn't give him the satisfaction of hearing it.

At the top of the stairs he said, "Now into the kitchen. Wipe that blood off your face."

"Why? So you can mess it up again?"

"Don't give me any sass. Do what I tell you."

"You busted my nose."

"Not yet—not enough blood. Next time I'll mash it to a pulp."

He was right about the blood: not as much dribbling out now. But the numbness had worn off and her nose had begun to throb like hell. Not broken, maybe, but some badly bruised cartilage. A few red drops plopped into the kitchen sink, swirled away when she turned on the cold-water tap. She soaked a dish towel, wiped the stickiness off her face and hands. Rinsed the towel and wet it again and held it gingerly against her nose.

"How'd you find out?" she said. "Who told you?"

"Who do you think?"

"Yeah. Doctor Easy."

"Too bad for you he didn't believe what the judge told him."

"Fool."

"Bedroom," he said.

"What?"

"You heard me."

"Why? You gonna rape me?"

He laughed, nasty. "Last thing on my mind. Had all of your chubby body I can stand—I don't need another lousy lay."

That made her even more coldly furious. Chubby body! Lousy lay!

"Go on," he said. "The bedroom."

"What for?"

"Keep things like scarves in there, don't you?"

"Scarves? What . . . tie me up?"

"You're not stupid; I'll give you that much."

"Tie me up and then what? Slice and dice?"

"No. Not here, anyway. We're going for a ride."

Those thin curls of fear rose again, and this time they didn't burn away. "Where?"

"You'll find out."

The hell I will, she thought. Not going anywhere with you, asshole. Tied up, helpless . . . no way!

The knife swayed again, like a snake's head. "Move."

She moved, into the hallway that led to the bedrooms. Hers, the master bedroom, was on the right. Just before she reached the open doorway, she stopped and leaned her shoulder heavily against the wall, loosening the press of her fingers on the wet dish towel.

He came up close beside her, nudged her with an elbow. "Move."

"Woozy," she said. "Give me a second. . . ."

He stepped over a little, almost in front of her. As soon as he did that she pivoted off the wall, swung the dish towel in an arc against the side of his face, then slapped it down over the hand holding the knife and let go of it. At the same time she kicked him in the shin as hard as she could. He yelled, stumbled, bounced off the opposite wall.

Before he could recover, she was inside the bedroom. Slamming the door, twisting the dead-bolt lock.

He yelled again out there, pounded on the door, and shook

the knob and hollered something she didn't pay attention to. By then she was across the room, at the glass doors that opened out onto a tiny balcony. She unlocked the doors, quick, and threw them open; chill, damp air swirled into the room.

The uphill house next door, close across an areaway, showed dark all along this side. Wouldn't do any good to stand out there yelling for help, just waste time. It was a long drop from the balcony to the strip of hard ground below. A drainpipe ran down from the roof on one side; you could shinny down that . . . somebody could, but not her. Afraid of heights, had been all her life. No good at clinging and climbing, either—that kind of athletic stuff had never been her thing.

She didn't hesitate more than a couple of seconds before she pivoted and ran across to the big walk-in closet, the soft-pile carpet muffling the sound of her steps.

"Bitch! You can't get away from me!"

Hurling himself at the door now, trying to break it in. Fairly thick and the lock wasn't flimsy, but how long would it hold?

The closet had a pair of louvered folding doors that she kept open. Once she was inside, she pulled them closed. In the darkness she felt her way to the back wall—all bureaulike drawers built in beneath where the pitch of the roof sloped inward at a low angle. In the ceiling just in front of the draw-ers was the trapdoor that gave access to the attic. She was just tall enough to reach the panel by standing on tiptoe, to slide it open in its metal frame.

Yelling, frenzied thumping out there in the hall—he hadn't busted the lock yet. Maybe he wouldn't; maybe it was strong enough to keep him out. . . .

There was a button mounted just inside the trap opening. A stretch and she found it, pressed it. The short set of aluminum steps unfolded electronically from inside a set of brackets, making a low whirring sound as they came down on a slant—a sound that got lost in the noise Delman was making. She went up the steps as fast and quiet as she could, scrambled over onto the storage platform to the left.

Another button was set into a stud up there. And a switch for a couple of overhead bulbs, but she didn't dare put on the lights. She felt around until she found the ladder button. The low whir came again; the steps started to wind up next to her.

Loud crash below. The lock hadn't held.

He was in the bedroom now.

Tamara scooted around to lie flat on her belly, then leaned down into the opening to try to slide the trapdoor panel back into place. Couldn't quite reach it; the frame for the stairs was in the way. If he came into the closet, turned on the light, saw the open trap—

She told herself that wouldn't happen. First things he'd see were the wide open balcony doors and he'd head straight over there, go out onto the balcony, look over the railing. Think she'd managed to shinny down the drainpipe, was on her way for help, and haul his ass out of here in a hell of a hurry. And she'd wait ten minutes to make sure he was gone, then go on down and call the cops and that'd be the end of Antoine fucking Delman.

Tamara wiggled backward on the platform. A spiderweb brushed her face; she swiped it off. The attic's damp mustiness seemed to wrap itself around her. She could feel it on her skin as she lay listening.

Silence down there.

Still out on the balcony, trying to spot her in the dark? Come on, you son of a bitch, I'm long gone. Get the hell out!

Something wet dripped onto the back of her hand.

Sweat . . . no, blood. Her nose was bleeding again from the exertion, throbbing like the worst toothache she'd ever had. Another drop fell, and another—

Oh, shit—what if it'd been bleeding again *before* she came up here? What if she'd left a trail of blood drops across the bedroom to the closet? But she hadn't, she hadn't, and even if she had he wouldn't notice—

Yeah, she had.

Yeah, he did.

The louvered closet doors rattled open. A second later the light came on.

Fear, a knot of it this time, rose up in her throat. She pulled farther away from the platform's edge, into the musty darkness, the rough boards scraping her palms. The platform was about a dozen feet long and narrow, empty except for a handful of items the former tenants had left behind; she hadn't had the time or inclination to clean it out, move her own storage stuff up here. Only been in the attic once before, with the rental agent on her first look at the flat. The rest of it was exposed rafters and joists and crosspieces, and mounds of insulation like dirty saffron-colored snow puffed up between the joists. No place to hide, no window or any other way out.

"I know you're up there, bitch. Better come on down."

She lay still, holding her breath, cursing herself. All that time with Pop getting herself firearms certified . . . wasted because she'd been too busy, too lazy, too stupid to buy a handgun. If she had, she'd've kept it in her nightstand drawer and none of this would be happening—

"Make me come up there after you, I'll cut you into little pieces."

Couldn't go down to him, couldn't, couldn't! He'd use that knife on her no matter what she did. The fury behind the pretend calm in his voice told her that.

"All right, you asked for it."

She heard him leave the closet, then faint sounds in the bedroom she couldn't identify.

A weapon . . . anything up here she could use? Frantically she felt along the dusty boards, trying to remember what the former tenants had left behind and where it was. Wicker laundry basket. Roll of moldy rattan window shades that would probably crumble to dust if you picked them up. Box of old sheets and towels. Maybe she could . . . no, forget it. No hope of unfolding a sheet and throwing it over him in this dark cramped space, wouldn't be enough time anyway.

She heard him come back into the closet. Heard him fumbling around inside the trapdoor opening, trying to figure out how to get the ladder down.

What else was here? Sharp object, or a heavy one like a chair or small table? Dammit, no, nothing like that.

It didn't take him long to find the button. The low whirring came again; the steps began to unfold downward.

Jesus, sweet Jesus. She squirmed farther away from the edges of light, sweeping her hands over the platform now like a blind person. Something, anything . . . nothing but dust and dried mouse turds.

The whirring stopped; the ladder was all the way down.

She felt a sudden crazy urge to give up, curl herself into a ball, like one of those little bugs when they were about to be squashed. The hell with that! She kept moving, kept sweeping, the dust clogging her throat and aching nose, her breath coming in little muffled gasps.

A spear of light shot up through the trap opening, steadied and made a yellow-white circle on one of the rafters. Flashlight beam. That was what he'd been doing in the bedroom, looking for a flashlight, and he'd found the one she kept in the nightstand.

Her hand touched something . . . the wicker basket. Pushed it away. Touched something else, something that rolled and rattled.

Delman was on the stairs now, starting up.

She caught hold of the rolling thing—a round, smooth piece of wood. Remembered what it was just before her fingers confirmed it.

Closet clothes pole!

Her pulse rate surged. Up on her knees then, quick and quiet, lifting the pole with both hands and pulling it across her body. Felt like it was about three feet long, not heavy but solid.

The flash beam roamed over the cobwebby rafters and studs, but it couldn't reach to where she was; the angle was wrong. He'd have to come most of the way up before he could swing it around in her direction.

There was enough room along the platform so a person of her height could stand upright without banging her head on one of the rafters. She pushed onto her feet, hunched over with the clothes pole tight against her chest, her hands sliding down to one end until she was gripping it like a baseball bat.

Delman's head appeared in the opening, then his upper body. The cone of light wobbled and danced lower over the skeletal timbers, making pieces of them appear and disappear in the heavy blackness.

She crept forward, turning her body, praying there'd be nothing in the way when she swung the pole.

He came up the last step; shifted the yellow ray toward her as he turned onto the platform, the light glinting off the blade of the knife in his other hand.

Two quick steps and she whipped the pole at the shape of him with all her strength.

He heard her and the swish of the pole—too late. Nothing got in the way of the swing; the end of the pole hit him high up on the body and sent him reeling sideways, howling. He slammed into one of the studs with enough force to shake the platform and make him lose the knife—she heard it drop and bounce metallically as he caromed off, teetered on the platform's edge.

Tamara swung again and this time her aim was better: smacked him hard upside the head, a solid impact that tore the pole out of her grasp and the flashlight out of his. All the smacking, clattering sounds combined to create hollow rolling echoes; the torch swirled light like a pinwheel. She saw him twist, flail, topple backward, and fall onto the exposed joists. A scream tore out of him as soon as he landed—must've broken something, because he couldn't stop himself from rolling down between two of the joists, into and through the puffs of fiberglass insulation.

Another strangled shriek, then a loud thud that choked it off. After that, only a thick, charged silence.

Tamara let out her cramped breath in a little sob of relief. The flashlight had stayed on the platform; it was rolling from side to side, casting long yellow arcs. She picked it up. The adrenaline rush was fading now; her hand shook so badly she had to take a double grip to hold the light steady. At the platform's edge, she aimed the beam at the spot where he'd fallen. She could just see him down there, all twisted up, not moving.

Lord of mercy, she thought.

Her wobbly legs carried her to the ladder, down it through the closet and bedroom into the hallway. Filmy white dust in the air there, filtering out of the dining room. Plaster dust.

She looked in through the doorway. More dust and pieces of plaster littering the floor, the ceiling cracked and bulging where the weight of Delman's body had crashed into it. Damn wonder he hadn't busted all the way through, be lying here on the floor with that plaster dust all over him. Black punk in white-face.

Landlord's gonna be pissed, she thought. Probably make me pay to have the ceiling fixed.

Laughter, the wild kind, bubbled up in her; she clamped her jaws tight to keep it in. If she let it out, she knew she might not be able to stop.

27

JAKE RUNYON

It was late, almost ten, by the time he got to Bryn's house. He'd called her from Ullman's, while they were waiting for the Daly City police, and she still wanted to see him tonight, no matter how late it was. Did he mind? No, he didn't mind. Not tonight, not anytime. She didn't even need a reason; all she had to do was ask.

"You look tired," she said when she let him in.

So did she. Tired and stressed out. Drinking again, too. She wasn't drunk or even high, but he could smell the wine on her breath and her eyes wore a slight glaze.

He said, "I can use a cup of tea."

"I'll put the kettle on. Bad night?"

"Bad enough." That was all he'd say about it. And she wouldn't ask any more. She understood that he didn't like to talk about his work, preferred to compartmentalize his personal and professional lives. Even if that weren't the case, he wouldn't have told her what he'd seen in Zachary Ullman's bedroom, what had happened out there tonight. Child porn was a highly emotional issue with just about everybody, all the more so for a psychologically fragile mother with a nine-year-old son who'd been taken away from her.

Neither of them said much until the tea was ready and she'd poured another glass of wine for herself and they were on the couch in the living room. She brooded into her glass for a little time before she said, "What happened today . . . I don't like burdening you with it, but I need to talk to someone, someone who'll understand."

"What happened?"

"Bobby came to school with a fractured arm. The principal called me when he couldn't get hold of Robert."

"The boy okay?"

"His arm, yes. It's not a bad fracture—hairline crack of the ulna."

"How'd it happen?"

"He said he fell on his way to school."

"Said he fell? You don't believe him?"

"I don't know what to believe," Bryn said. "He wouldn't talk about it, wouldn't look me in the eye. And he didn't tell anyone at school, classmates or teachers. One of the teachers found out when another boy pushed him in the hall and he yelled and clutched his arm."

"You think somebody hurt him and he's covering up? Older kids, a schoolyard bully?"

"That's one possibility. But he's usually friendly, outgoing, the kind of boy everybody likes and gets along with."

"Usually?"

"I told you how Bobby was with me last weekend. Quiet, withdrawn—not like himself at all. I wanted to believe it was just a phase, but now . . . I think it's more serious than that. More serious than other kids pushing him around."

Runyon said nothing for a time. Then, "His father?"

"Yes. It isn't just the fractured arm, Jake. When I took Bobby to the doctor, he didn't want to take off his shirt so they could put a soft cast on his arm. We made him do it. His back and shoulders . . . bruises, lots of them."

Christ. "What did he say?"

"He said he got them playing football. But he was lying—I could see it in his eyes. He got those bruises at home."

"You never mentioned physical abuse before."

"There wasn't any while Robert and I were married. I'd swear to that. He's a controlling, vindictive shit, but I never imagined he was an abuser, too. If I had . . . my God, I'd've used it against him at the custody hearing."

"Why would he change, start hurting Bobby?"

"I don't know. Financial problems, trouble with his practice or with this woman he's planning to marry . . . I just don't know. But I'm afraid he has."

"Did you talk to him today?"

"Yes. He was home when I took Bobby there from the doctor's."

"Accuse him?"

"Not in so many words. I said I thought somebody was hurting Bobby; he said he didn't believe it. Refused to discuss the matter. There was something about the way he acted . . . evasive. That damn glib lawyer evasiveness. You know?"

"I know."

"If I did accuse him, he'd just deny it—and make me out to be paranoid for even suggesting such a thing. I don't know what to do, Jake. What can I do if Bobby won't admit the truth?"

"Talk to him again, try to convince him."

264 • Bill Pronzini

"I don't think I can get through to him. He won't tell on his father. Robert's too controlling—Bobby's afraid of him."

Runyon was silent.

Bryn tried to gulp some of her wine instead of sipping it with the good side of her mouth. Some of it spilled out, down the front of her robe. She said, "Shit!" and then, when Runyon started to reach out to her, "No, don't. Don't." She mopped up the spilled wine with the hem of the robe in quick, angry movements.

He waited, not saying anything, letting her pick up the conversation when she was ready.

"I'm terrified it'll get worse," she said, "worse than a fractured arm. If anything really bad happens to Bobby . . . I couldn't stand that, I can barely cope with things the way they are now."

Runyon said slowly, "Maybe there's something I can do."

"I'm not asking for your help; I wouldn't ask. Support, advice . . . that's all."

"Not enough, if you're right about the abuse."

"I'm right, but . . . it's not the kind of domestic situation a private detective can investigate; we both know that."

"Officially, no."

"There's nothing you could do anyway. You don't know Robert, how spiteful he is, the way he uses the law like a weapon. You'd only end up getting hurt."

"Not if he's guilty."

"Jake . . . please. Don't get involved."

Runyon was thinking about what he'd seen tonight in Ullman's bedroom. Different kind of child abuse, but abuse nonetheless. Little kids being hurt by adults without conscience or humanity.

"I already am," he said.

28

Kerry said, her voice thick with disgust, "It must have been like walking into a chamber of horrors."

"Pretty close. What the cops found on Ullman's computer and in those scrapbooks was even worse than what was on the walls. There must've been five thousand individual images, plus more than a hundred videos."

"My God. How long has he been wallowing in it?"

"Fifteen years. Started while he was still married."

"Is that why his wife divorced him?"

"No," I said. "He was careful about keeping it hidden from her. Joe Hoffman wasn't careful at all. Kept his collection in his workshop where his wife stumbled on it. He didn't have much back then, just a batch of photos that she burned without thinking."

"How could Ullman keep all his garbage out in the open like he did . . . blown-up photographs on the walls in plain sight? Somebody might've walked in there by accident. Or did he want to get found out?"

"I think he did. He confessed readily enough. But he protected himself pretty well just the same. Has no friends, male or female, never invited anybody to his house except other sickos like Hoffman."

"Hoffman was his supplier?"

"One of them. They were part of a Bay Area cell—buying, selling, trading with one another."

Kerry pulled her robe more tightly around herself. We were in our bedroom with the door shut, talking in low voices. Emily was either in bed or still doing homework—I hadn't checked when I came in a few minutes before—and probably listening to music on her iPod. But we weren't taking any chances.

"The police found a dozen names on Ullman's computer," I said. "There'll be a lot more arrests in the next few days."

"Well, I hope Ullman rots in prison for the rest of his life."

"Not much chance of that. He's in a pretty bad way—guilt, remorse, self-loathing. I won't be surprised if he ends up in a psychiatric facility."

"You believe him that he never actually . . . you know, harmed a child?"

"If he ever did, he'll confess to it eventually. But I doubt it. He's a voyeur and a coward, and it's a good bet he was molested by somebody as a child, but I don't see him as a molester himself. Except in his imagination."

"He's a monster just the same."

"No argument there."

"Visualizing himself with all those poor kids in the photos?" Kerry made a faint gagging sound. "With the kids he taught at Whitney? With *Emily*?"

I didn't say anything.

"She liked and trusted him—one of her favorite teachers. Protected him, for God's sake. And the whole time . . ."

"Easy," I said. "Don't go there."

"I can't help it. It makes me want to vomit."

"Emily thought she was doing the right thing. She's young; she believes people are basically good and honest and authority figures don't lie."

"She'll be devastated when she finds out."

"For a while. But she'll get over it."

"I don't want her to find out at school, from the other kids. We'll have to tell her."

"First thing in the morning."

"It won't be easy."

"It was a lot harder telling her what happened to her birth mother. She survived that—she'll survive this, too."

"So much pain in her life," Kerry said. "Only thirteen, and all that ugliness and betrayal. She's such a good kid, she deserves so much better."

"I know."

"I wish we could protect her the way she protected Ullman. Keep any more of the ugliness from hurting her."

"We can try," I said. "That's all any parent can do—try."

29

TAMARA

For a while the place was a madhouse. Uniformed cops, inspectors, EMTs, even a couple of firemen with axes. Delman had busted his ankle in the fall; they had to cut him moaning out of the dining room ceiling. Her nose had fared better. Sore and a little swollen, but not broken. Lucky. Down the line tonight—lucky.

She'd told the inspectors everything she knew about Antoine and Alisha and their con game, along with everything that had happened tonight. Hadn't kept any of the victims' names out of it. Hadn't spared herself, either—fessed up her motives for going after the Delmans. Talked and answered questions until her mouth and throat were so dry she had to keep pouring down glasses of water, which only made her have to call time-out while she went in to pee.

The last of them were gone now and she was all juiced out, physically and mentally. What she wanted was a hot bath and about ten hours' sleep. But not here, not tonight. Broken laths and plaster all over the dining room, some of that white dust still in the air. Flashes of the rage and terror she'd felt up there in the dark attic giving her the jimjams. A too-quiet stillness that had already begun to press down on her like a heavy weight.

She got her coat and car keys and beat it out of there.

Could've gone to Bill and Kerry's, Vonda and Ben's, some of her other friends, but then she'd've been stuck with another round of Q & A and she wasn't up to that. When in doubt, pick on your nearest relative, even if it's one you've had a prickly relationship with all your life. So that was where she went, to sister Claudia on Telegraph Hill—Tel Hi, the residents were calling it now, stupid name.

Claudia was in bed when Tamara got there—alone, fortunately. Her Oreo boyfriend, another lawyer like her, had his own crib; he'd been trying to get her to move in with him, but she kept saying no, she didn't want to give up her independence. Why anyone would want to live with Claudia was beyond Tamara. Girl was a born-again vegan, wouldn't eat anything that wasn't grown organically and scrubbed in purified water, had about as much sense of humor as a duck, refused to own a TV set, and spent her spare time reading obscure law precedents.

She'd also inherited Pop's sigh when dealing with her "difficult" little sister. She let loose three or four of them when Tamara told her she needed a place to crash for the night, she'd explain why in the morning. But Claudia didn't argue or lecture, as she might've done some other time. Didn't call her Tammie, either, a name she hated as much as Pop's Sweetness and wouldn't've put up with tonight. Claudia could be a pain in the ass sometimes, but she was a rock when it came to family unity. She cared in her own tight-assed way. Vice versa, though Tamara didn't go around admitting it.

The guest room had a private bath. She soaked in a hot tub for half an hour, then swallowed three Tylenol and crawled between cool sheets. Was sure she'd be able to sleep right away, but it didn't happen. Still too wired. Thoughts and emotions and flash images kept tumbling around inside her head.

So it was over, finished. The Delmans were going down— payback complete, and a good deed done besides, even if Judge Mantle and Doctor Easy didn't agree. Revenge is sweet, right?

Then how come she felt low again? How come the taste was more bitter than sweet?

Somebody'd said that it was like eating a skimpy meal: you wanted it bad and it went down pretty easy when you got it, but it didn't fill you up; it didn't satisfy you for long. Yeah. Could be.

Could also be emotional wipeout. You couldn't go through what she'd gone through tonight without a bad reaction. Happened that way twice before, hadn't it? The Christmas hostage thing in the old agency offices and the kidnapping nightmare in the East Bay. The high might come back again tomorrow and last for a while. And every time she looked back on this week in her life she'd smile, feel satisfied and vindicated.

Maybe.

And maybe the high wouldn't come again; maybe she'd be looking back and wondering if she hadn't been six kinds of fool, and a lucky fool at that, to let herself get caught up in a personal vendetta that'd almost cost her her life.

She knew what Claudia would say when she found out, the same thing she'd said any number of times before. "When are you going to grow up, Tamara? When are you going to get wise to yourself?" She'd scoffed at that before because she'd always thought she had grown up, was wise to herself. Wrong?

No.

Yes.

Anyhow, she'd learned some things, some hard lessons. About men and relationships, about professional ethics and self-protection, about herself. One thing for sure: she wouldn't make the same mistakes twice.

JUN - - 2010